The Battle for Billabong Balagh

Evil lives in those who hate.
Time to rise and face your fate.
Within yourself a bravery unknown.
Time to rise and protect your home.

Travel harsh lands with hearts laid bare.
Open to love and all that is fair.
When the time comes to open your soul.
Bravery, Integrity and Loyalty be foretold.

Thulo

2

ISBN: 978-1-7642314-0-4 (Paperback)

ISBN: 978-1-7642314-1-1 (ebook)

A catalogue record for this book is available from the National Library of Australia

Publisher – Robert Harrington

Cover Artist – Karen Roberts

Chapters

Terminology used by our epic adventurers.

1. ***Tall Walkers*** - Kangaroo name for humans

2. ***Stealth Walkers*** - Kangaroo name for dingoes

3. ***Billabong*** - A branch off a river forming a backwater or pool by water flowing from the river during a flood.

4. ***Boab*** - Known as the bottle tree (due to its shape) or the tree of life

5. ***Lizard*** - Characterised by having legs, moveable eyelids, scales and external ears

6. ***Ghosting's*** - Game played between the kangaroos where they hide at sunset and must remain hidden until sunrise. They are pursued by a chosen player and if caught have a stripe of mud from the billabong placed down their snout. Those found are displayed (mud and all) in front of the rest of the community to add further embarrassment

7. ***Kookaburra*** - Kookaburras are terrestrial tree kingfishers of the genus Dacelo native to Australia and New Guinea. The loud distinctive calls of the laughing Kookaburra are often used as a stock sound effect when films are made around the Australian bush setting.

8. ***Greys*** - Refers to the grey kangaroo and grey refers to the colour of their fur. They on average weight 66kg with a height of 3ft 7 inches to 4ft 3 inches.

9. ***Reds*** - Refers to the red kangaroo and red refers to the colour of their fur. They on average weight 90kg with a height of 5ft 10 inches.

10. ***Roo's*** - Human shortened word for Kangaroos

11. ***Troop*** - A collective group of kangaroos

Northern Threat Rising

The gap in the high rock wall was their only weak point for the planned attack. Broadback licked his gnarled scar to moisten the tough skin that lay across the bridge of his snout as he stared into the intense deep-set brown eyes of his most trusted friend.

"The time is coming," said Broadback in his quiet, gravelled voice as he turned to face the vast open plain that billowed out before him.

The vastness splayed out before the community of Balagh was unfathomable. Across the red plain sat sporadic clumps of tall, wide-spanning trees whose thin long leaves shadowed the low-lying thick, whispery scrub that crowded their lower trunks in desperate search of shade. The clumped thin shoots sprouted from the thick boles gently wafted in the early morning breeze. The sheer vastness gave no point of reference from which to gauge any meaningful distance across the mottled canvas of orange, red and yellow..

The glare radiating from the sand when the sun was at its highest, resulted in any viewer having to squint to admire its bleak, beautiful harshness.

For those who accepted its gentle whispered invitation to simply wander with abandonment, without adequate provision, would likely die a lonely death with only thirst, hallucinations and starvation to accompany them in their dying screams.

From the shadows of the large cave, Broadback stared down at Tronta, an orange glow reflecting off his single laser blue eye as the half-orbed sun sat on the distant horizon.

"I have been made aware of a recent meeting and a massing of the greys and reds far to the north," turning to stare into the distant shimmer.

Tronta followed Broadback's gaze. "I will assemble the troops," he growled after a momentary pause. "I will set up watches, further add to our defences and prepare for our departure."

Broadback said nothing, his silence and unrelenting stare enough for Tronta to move off and join the large group of battle-hardened boomers who were gathered at the water's edge in anticipation of the outcome of the meeting between their King and their second-in-command.

Thulo stood motionless in the deep shadows of a cave with his stare firmly set on his father, Broadback, while he spoke to Tronta. Thulo had seen a similar look of concentration on his father's face before but sensed there was something different on this occasion. His father seemed troubled, the weight of responsibility and uncertainty clearly etched across his face. As he pondered the right time to approach his father, Thulo noticed the furless scar that sat prominent across his snout and down into his neck, glowed orange and red and pulsed deep in the early morning sun. It was if this was a further beacon they were in imminent danger. Sensing the time was right, Thulo hopped quietly along his father's long, broad shadow to the raised rocky ledge upon which he now stood alone. Each hop was purposeful to avoid interrupting his father's concentrated stare. On approaching his father's side, he stopped and stood in respectful silence.

In the void of words, he found himself subconsciously puffing out his chest and straightening his spine to his fullest height which took him to his father's shoulder. He gritted his teeth to pulse into life his mandible muscles which tightened and widened his jawline. With the transformation complete, he felt considerably more intimidating and older than his years. In the continued silence, he followed his father's gaze to the distant shimmer and although the scene was beautiful, he wondered what his father stared at with such intensity.

Within his thoughtless silence, his eyes slowly drifted to two squabbling egrets. Both stood with long thin spindly legs, separated midway by hinged knees that sat just above the water in the nearby billabong. They were squabbling loudly as each pulled from the opposite ends of a now dead fish, both eager for the reward of food and dominance over the other. As Thulo's cheeks rose into a smile at the scene, his father's voice broke like a sudden lightning strike, bringing him back to reality with a crack. He stood bolt upright with a start, the natural slouch that had slowly infiltrated his spine, straightened. He peered up and took particular noticed at how broad and chiselled his father's chest, shoulders and arms were and sensed the aura of potential menace that surrounded him. His father still faced north when he began to speak.

"I am sending Tronta on a twofold mission. First, to enhance our defences at the arch to the north and to meet the kings from the south and the west with their respective battle-ready boomers." Each word was purposeful and quiet, but each delivered with an edge that immediately gripped Thulo's attention.

When his father paused, Thulo knew the second part of the mission would be the one that held the greatest danger.

"We will soon be at war, Thulo, with those who wish to do us harm; those who go by the name of the north Raider. They are a brutal mob, driven by vengeance and greed and led by their self-appointed leader, Clais, the son of King Krage. After a short pause Broadback, who was now into his strategic stride added, "I want you to go and stand side-by-side with your brothers."

Thulo opened his mouth to speak, closed it, only to open it again and clear his throat before repeating what he thought he had heard. "You want me to go, north?" His voice crackled with uncertainty, although his pitch was intended to be one of positivity, bravery and excitement.

"Yes, Thulo," Broadback answered now looking at him, his blue eye twinkling as though he recognised the veiled trepidation in his son's voice. "Thulo, there has never in our history been a greater direct threat to our way of life than there is now. A threat to the freedoms we have strived to build and share with those who we love and those from outside of Balagh's great walls who we call our friends. The darkness that masses to the north, if victorious, will ravage and destroy the very foundations of everything we hold dear. As my son, it's expected you will stand and face the challenge. To protect Balagh's freedoms and all those who live here as part of your family heritage and future legacy.

Broadback turned and looked up at the high wall in the cave. "Your forefathers have been etched on the sacred wall. Each stand side-by-side as pillars of sacrifice and leadership that have afforded over generations the freedoms, prosperity and safety we enjoy and cherish to this very day. This is now your time, as my son, to confront our biggest threat and in doing so understand who you really are. This response to the threat will give you the opportunity to gain experience, learn and observe, make decisions and likely at times make mistakes. Yes, make mistakes," he repeated when he noted Thulo's eyes widen. "And for each mistake, or decision made, having the courage to embrace the learnings from time given to self-reflection. The opportunity for self-growth in the most troublesome of times should be grasped by both paws. Never be afraid to face adversity or embrace weakness. Each presents its own unique opportunity to learn and should not be seen negatively but as an unrehearsed blessing. With each experience you face a unique opportunity to learn, in both the good, and more importantly, the bad." With a smile, he turned to face north again.

"You will travel with Gribe, who will lead alongside Tronta." After a momentary pause, Broadback suddenly looked stern and turned to face Thulo. He placed his heavy front paws on Thulo's shoulders. "You will be expected to fight, my son," his father said sternly, his blue eye now sharp and focused. "You will fight alongside Tronta and Gribe as you have practised and you must not leave their side. Do. Not. Leave. Them," he reiterated as his stare intensified, so much so, Thulo fought hard to hold it. "If your life is in imminent danger and those who are committed to defend you cannot, you must retreat and return to me with haste. Do you understand?" His grip intensified on Thulo's shoulder.

Thulo nodded, "I do," deciphering what he meant by this statement. His stomach suddenly started to squirm as if he had swallowed a fish that was very much alive and fighting hard to find its way back out again.

With this his father turned to look back with a squinted stare into the dry shimmer.

Thulo however continued to stare at his father. It was as if the very tip of his strong tail was a fuse which had now been lit. The heat raced quickly up and over each and every nodule in his spine before ending in a puff of multi-coloured lights deep within his brain.

The moisture in his mouth was drying twice as quick as normal as his jaw hung slightly ajar on its hinge. He turned to look north in pounding silence. The landmarks that had become so familiar in his normal everyday life now appeared to be three times further away. He frowned through squinting eyes. The sun hovered silent and motionless on the horizon as if a thief not wanting to make a noise. It was if its back was turned while it eavesdropped on their conversation and didn't want to leave until the conversation had finished. On hearing the news of Thulo's inclusion to head north, the sun seemed only too happy to focus its last remaining light in a concentrated beam on where he was about to travel. Thulo continued to stare, although unseeing as his thoughts were awash with excitement and apprehension with regards to the task his father, the King, had bestowed upon him.

The following evening Thulo sat in solitude high and hidden on a wide flat plateau. His large hind legs splayed out at the hip; his upper body supported on his short thick muscular tail.

His powerful lower half allowed Thulo and his kin to hop with large bounds, covering distances quickly with pace and surprising agility. At the end of his long hind paws sat a large singular claw, which, in conjunction with his large powerful tail, would allow him to sit back and gauge any would-be attacker. The remaining two claws fused as one, their purpose solely for grooming and leaning upon when hopping slowly and foraging.

In contrast, his upper body was less wide but equally powerful across the shoulders and chest. The fur was soft and thick, affording protection. Thulo's fur was a hazelnut red although the colour of the fur varied depending on their location of birth and generally lay between red and grey. Like all of his kin, regardless of fur colour his eyes and ears which were highly attuned, allowed them to see, smell and hear across a great distance, a distinct advantage to escape or prepare for any would-be threat.

Thulo sat staring at a small rock which peaked out of the sand. Within his periphery three busy ants were scurrying quickly across the cooling sand with legs moving in unison triumphantly carrying a large upturned deceased insect. They travelled quickly, their hooked claws at the end of their segmented limbs were not immune to the heat. Each grain of sand he assumed must have appeared as a large rock in their domed mirrored eyes. The hole to their nest approached and led steeply to their industrious nest, a network of tunnels filled with hungry mouths deep below the sand and rock. Upon arrival at the opening, the ants worked skilfully to manoeuvre the prize to the exact angle to that of the irregular shaped entrance. Thulo looked away as the final problem joint was unceremoniously straightened and with a final unified pull, they disappeared into the descending darkness.

His solitary thoughts on his discussion with his father were subconsciously broken by the sound of small stones and rocks sliding on soil somewhere behind him. The heavier boulders tumbled with considerable speed, each ricocheting off each other in their newfound freedom. Strangely, Thulo's thoughts, albeit brief, entertained the idea that each object was alive as if each tumbling rock hoped to be the first to reach the cooling water of the nearby billabong upon which they had looked upon from up high for an eternity. He imagined each one stopping abruptly at the base of the steep bank upon impact. Their weight absorbed into the thick unforgiving sand and with that their dreams ended.

At this he gazed in the direction of the solitary entrance to the plateau. A pair of large brown twinkling eyes, set above a broad grin with pointed pulsing whiskers, appeared, all framed within an excited face.

"Here you are," said Whisper with a lisp, her tongue visible as it contorted to create the words.

"Yeah, I needed some time to think alone," said Thulo as Whisper, his sister, bounded towards him. "I had a talk with father earlier." He paused with his mouth open, which dried quickly before he continued. "Father wants me to travel north with Tronta and Gribe to battle the north raiders. He wants me to go to war." His voice rose in pitch with each word.

Whisper stood next to him, staring up. Thulo noted her tongue was motionless although her mouth was open and poised, as if to speak. Her narrowed eyes were ablaze with a defiant stare and seemed to speak on her mouth's behalf.

"That's brilliant," she stammered after a prolonged pause, her voice quavering but with an undertone of annoyance. Her tongue, although continuing to move, formed no further words.

"What's wrong?" he asked, confused at her unusual stance, which had now sagged with her whiskers drooped; the electricity and excitement in her eyes now dull.

"It's so frustrating," she blurted, stomping her paw on the ground before turning her back on him.

A nearby lizard basking on a rock, jumped from its stupor at the sudden noise. With its tongue flicking in annoyance, it scurried off to find a safe dark under-hang where it would wait quietly before starting its nocturnal hunt. Dusk was fast approaching as the sun's final light faded and the silvery shadows crept forward like a silent thief of light under the moon's watchful eye.

"It's so frustrating," Whisper repeated with her back turned. "I will never get such a chance to prove myself, go on an adventure, do something meaningful." Her voice trailed off.

Thulo studied his sister's back where a cooling breeze suddenly wafted through her soft short fur. He noted how, although her outer coat was tipped by brown and black was underpinned by a bed of the purist white. He approached Whisper in silence and hopped to stand by her side; their long shadows joined as one as they were in life as twins. He glanced down at her slightly bowed head then lifted his eyes to the first twinkling stars. Each was set perfectly against the dark backdrop and he noted how they seemed far brighter than usual. As he peered into Whisper's eyes, he couldn't help but notice they were now dark and sunken. They were lifeless and he wondered if the moon had stolen Whisper's usual twinkles for her own.

"You're incredible," Thulo said, with a positive upbeat tone. "You are so brave and adventurous, the…"

"It's not enough, it will never be enough. There will never be a female leader." Whisper cut across him mid-sentence, her voice quavering but firm. "I will be here forever, living the expected life, to support, gather, mother - boring." With a long sigh, her exhaled breath whistled through her lisp.

Thulo opened his mouth to give a reply but paused and closed it again as he knew what she said to be true if the story of their forefathers within the deep cave was to be followed.

"Sorry," she said, turning to him with serious eyes. "This is a great opportunity for you." She suddenly inhaled deep, licked her lips, reached up and gripped his paws. "I'm sure father believes," she paused again, "that you are next in line to be king and I believe sending you on this dangerous mission is to test you, to prepare you, to give you visibility to all within Balagh," she said in a rush to avoid interruption.

Thulo took an involuntary gasp, his legs sagged at the joint and he suddenly felt sick. High on a rock, no more than four good hops away, sat the lizard who had re-appeared at the new voice and stared with interest. Bobbing on its small front legs, it caught Thulo's attention. As they stared at each other, Thulo, much to his surprise, saw what he took to be a smile appear across the wide pointed scaly head. Its tongue flicked the cooling air rhythmically.

Thulo turned his eyes back to his sister. "What do you mean? Gribe is the next in line, he is the eldest." He hoped this argument would be the winning move to this ridiculous notion.

"Yes, but he is no leader. He is too centred, too closed. I love him as a brother and father loves him as a son, but he is, in my opinion, no king."

Thulo responded again with a deflecting point of fact. "Gribe is going - he is going on the task. He is leading the task." He hoped this new line of logic would derail her.

"Yes he is going, but think about it, Thulo," she said quickly in a tone of understanding calm. "I think father is sending him to support his belief that he is the natural heir. With an attack from the north raiders imminent, we need unity, not a family divided. A family that is strong in battle. I think father will tell him when the time is right, maybe after the battle is won and things settle."

Thulo's heart pumped fast and full. What she was saying could be plausible. As he worked through each permutation fighting hard to ignore the loud voice from deep within his cerebral cortex which screamed - run!

Whisper turned to face him, demanding his attention. "Thulo," she said firmly, "you're amazing, so grounded, loyal, caring and clever. You just don't see it. That's why Gribe treats you the way he does. He sees you as a threat, the only other viable king of Balagh."

The silence between them was thick with unspoken emotion. His mind spun like the whipping of sand into an ever-intensifying storm. It was powerful, purposeful and all-encompassing. Pictures flickered into life within the cylindrical vortex of the storm that raged. Whisper's face stretched long and faded in definition before disappearing completely. Memories whirled, each spinning quicker and quicker before his eyes. He instinctively closed them as the bright light, which was blinding on the outside, tried to prise them open with tiny hot fingers. Past images of family, friends, places and events became a flickering stream of colour. The voices within the vivid scenes were muffled in a hum of varied pitch and tone. Suddenly, he stopped dead with a jolt. His stomach lurched and he fought to keep the sloshing fluid deep within him contained. He instinctively firmed his stance and braced himself on his tail for fear of falling over.

He slowly opened his eyes. The unfolding scene was as though he was a bystander to the games he played with his father as a young joey. He hadn't seen it before, or noticed their underpinning point, until now. Each game watched was bound in laughter and with new clarity underpinned by education; each engineered to challenge his thoughts and beliefs. Each game instilled a desire to win, but with a measured response of thought, calculation, and reflection. He could clearly see the love in his father's face which was underpinned by a gentle knowing smile in where his young son's destiny lay.

On reflection, these games built the foundations from which he could build his future decisions but under the care and love and guidance of his father. He built networks of understanding, compassion, acceptance and tolerance to face an uncertain world.

Although he wanted to stay and be with his father, the memory faded and the spiral of colour and muffled sound whirled once more, before suddenly stopping again.

A new vision emerged: one that made his heart jolt, as he now stood with his mother, Olan. He was enveloped in her warm embrace and could smell her unique fragrance with which he had grown to love in her soft fur. Gently pushing him away, she gazed at him, as if passing a part of her soul through her tight grip and staring eyes; love, loyalty, understanding and compassion. Her teachings were soft, unscripted and as if a feather travelling freely on a gentle wind. However, this freedom allowed him to have self-exploration and abandonment of process. To think outside of the normal confines without prejudice or criticism.

He was suddenly prised from her embrace as the lights flickered once again. This time the vision was one of him talking with Filor, a friend of Whisper. He swallowed a deep gulp, that on its descending journey warmed his soul as he stood staring into her soft, twinkling hazel eyes. A warmth coursed through him as his heart pounded with a joyous rhythmic beat. A deep, warm sensation of all-encompassing protectiveness settled into his now clenched paws. He closed his eyes and knew this was the moment to tell Filor his true feelings. Feelings he had so long held secret. Feelings that had grown to be as big and as strong as the silver boab which sat at the far end of the billabong. This was the moment he had dreamt about, where they would become one and start a future together full of hope and happiness. With building excitement and trepidation, he slowly opened his eyes.

However, standing before him, was not Filor but his brother Gribe, whose eyes shone red as he was shouting at Thulo, prodding him in the chest and pointing at the ground upon which they both stood. Although no words could be heard, Gribe's posture and gestures were clearly one of anger and intense hatred. Thulo closed his eyes tighter than he had ever closed them before and prayed for the flicker to start again and take him far, far away.

On a large nearby rock, the scratching of the dancing lizard's claws penetrated his thoughts and brought him out of the vision he was having of his brother. Upon his return to reality, he instantly felt a waft of cool air that penetrated his fur to his underlying skin. The gentle breeze had entered the plateau clearing from somewhere beyond the huge V-shaped rocks that dominated the clearing with their sheer height and width. They stood as if two gatekeepers of the lands that lay far beyond the safety of the high surrounding walls that encircled Balagh.

Spying the concerned face of the lizard, he slowly absorbed and reflected upon what he had seen in the visions with flooding emotions. He stood with closed eyes, the weight initially felt from Filor's confession, now lifted.

'Hello,' said Whisper in a soft compassionate voice as if somehow recognizing that he had been on an emotional journey and one she wisely knew must not be interrupted.

He opened his eyes and they met instantly. He smiled and brought his sister into an all-encompassing embrace. Coughing, he loosened his grip and they both laughed as she falsely spluttered as if having been crushed.

Suddenly, they moved away from each other with an instinctive sensation of danger, as if they were being watched. Their ingrained twitch fibres tensed, each fibre ready and waiting for the command to either fight or take flight. There, looming out of the moon's dim glow, was Gribe. He hopped slowly along the narrow path. Each paw placed with precision to avoid any noise from a loosened rock or cracking twig from the small dry bushes that lined the track. The rock face on which he stood, had turned silvery grey with black pockets in its cragged depths of undulation. Gribe's fur contrast could not have been starker. Dark to his right within the shadow of the rock and to his left, almost silver in the moon's soft light. Thulo felt strangely betrayed. This was the same wall of rock, that only a few moons ago, had befriended him whilst playing 'ghostings' which cloaked him with its allegiance of invisibility.

"Dreaming again, Thulo?" Gribe said in a deep, slow voice. "You're going to have to wake up from your dream world if you are to join us in battle." His mouth opened just enough to say the words before closing it to clench his teeth. The muscles in his wide jaw protruded and recoiled, the grinding audible in the silence.

The lizard quickly turned on its smooth, flat purpose-built viewing platform, curious as to the new voice which had now entered the arena. It stilled and stared.

Gribe stopped some ten hops away from Thulo. He filled the narrowest point of the path, blocking the only exit from the opening. "I have spoken with father," he said. "He has briefed me on the requirement to fortify our defences and defend our home against the North Raiders." Gribe stared intently at Thulo, eyes unwavering and dark. "Father has further advised me that YOU are to accompany the troop," he said in a mocking tone. "I have been entrusted with your safety, to ensure you learn and be included." He prolonged the last word and paused, motionless, before opening his mouth again. "The group will take my lead and do as I say." The tone of the message, turned from informative to forceful in a menacing, whispered voice.

Thulo processed what had been said before speaking. He allowed a lengthy pause to defuse and transfer some of Gribe's asserted control. "Father asked me to join the group as a member of our family. I am not sure what I can offer but will do whatever is needed to protect our family and comrades for the greater good of our home." He did not mention Gribe's name or refer to him as one of the leaders of the troop. He spoke with a measured tone, unwavering and direct. The ensuing silence seemed to last an eternity as they stared at each other.

Gribe's narrowed stare was suddenly broken by a loud crunch that was so out of place in the silence, it demanded their attention.

The observing lizard, high on its platform, struggled to swallow the legs and wing of a large moth that had underestimated the length of the lizards whipping recoiling tongue.

Gribe, having processed what he had seen, returned his gaze to Thulo and Whisper. "I am returning to the cave, it's getting late and I have planning to do," he said in a dark, cold voice. After a momentary pause he turned and headed to the rock's edge. Before rounding the bend, he turned back. "This would make a great hiding place." He paused before disappearing into the darkness, the only indication of his presence the sound of the stones rolling down the bank as his weight dug deep.

Thulo immediately turned to face Whisper, afraid that what had been said between them had been overheard by Gribe while he stood silent and unseen in the shadows before making his appearance.

Whisper didn't offer any comfort. Her face showed the same concern, her mouth remaining closed before she swallowed deeply. As the night fell to its fullest, they cautiously headed back down to the billabong in the vain attempt of getting some sleep. Before departing, they agreed not to repeat what had been said between them. Any further conversations were only to be discussed when they were alone and on an agreed nod of their heads and a scratch to their right thigh if in company. Darkness engulfed them on rounding the bend.

The lizard sat alone; chest pushed high on straightened front legs. With a full stomach he turned and sluggishly scuttled off, reflecting on an evening of satisfying entertainment.

Life and Death

Far to the North the sons of the dead king, Krage, sat opposite the fires which danced shadows and light in an excited frenzy on either side of a large central rock. Motionless, they waited for Clais, the eldest of Krage's sons, and heir apparent, to take his place and face the triangular formation of smaller rocks that spanned out into a clearing amongst the tall trees that stood hushed in anticipation. The light from the other eleven fires lit the scene in a warm, welcoming glow, bringing each of the eleven ancient stones to life. Warmth, accompanied by an orange and yellow light, danced across their faces. Each offered a different tone, dependant on their hierarchical place as each stone descended in size, largest to smallest from the main central one. But what did not differ was the dark cold shadows cast over every stone to their rear. The most distal stone, and the smallest, lay at the point of the triangle, some twenty hops opposite to where Clais would sit and face his audience. The largest, and most imposing rock, stood noticeably elevated over all the others. Within the triangular formation, four stones remained vacant. The sons of Krage filled the rest. They sat in silence, heads slightly bowed and paws facing outwards as a sign of loyalty. Their long bony paws protruded out in front of them, with their claws dug deep into the sand like anchors. Each of Clais' brothers rested back on their thick muscular tails, ready to bear arms if so requested.

Out of the darkness, Clais loomed large. Heavy pawed, his jet-black fur shone like thick armour. His deep-set eyes were as black as the night sky which blanketed them above. A large white lower fang protruded over cushioned scar tissue, which was rolled and jagged where his lip should have been. The deformity had been inflicted during the fight that claimed his father's life. Taking his place at the largest of the stones, he sat alone without speaking. In the ensuing silence, his shadow shifted and changed shape as the fires on either side of the biggest and most dominant rock, competed to create the most distorted shadow. Stationary, he caught the eye of each of his brothers and held it for a few seconds. His eyes reflected the flames which mirrored simmering anger. He finally stared at Blont to his left, the second eldest and most trusted brother, who had not bowed but waited for Clais to speak.

After a momentary pause, Clais peered skywards and Blont spoke. "Speak the words."

At this, his brothers stood to attention and spoke in unison, "We will rise again with anger and hate when the sun lays bare the path we shall take. We will ravage the land, taking back what is ours, laying down routes for our brothers to travel. Revenge will be ours and written in blood for all those to remember the lives that were taken. For the day shall come when Clais will reign, and those who don't follow will be cast aside or slain." On finishing they sat.

Three others, who stood silent in the periphery, moved forward under escort. Two of the three were kings from distant mobs to the high north, the third was Shroud, a trusted friend of Clais. They took their positions at the remaining stones. Clais remained silent and unmoved as they settled.

Once seated, Clais looked at each in turn. "The time has come, brothers, for us to rise and take revenge for our father, the rightful King of these lands, and take back what is ours and to rid the land of the weak whom infest our most valuable resource, water."

Those in attendance remained silent, although they shuffled on the stones in adoration and agreeance.

"My father, the king, was tricked by Broadback when offered peace and in discussion about a fair settlement. He was brutally slain, dying a long and painful death. However, my father, the bravest of all those who wanted nothing more than peace and harmony, managed to land a final blow to his coward murderer before his life was taken. The strike, all powerful like him, took Broadback's eye and almost his life. To this day, Broadback remembers my father in that deep dark, disfigured socket as continued reminder of the betrayal and cowardly lie he lives."

There was a long pause. "Broadback brought shame on this family and has the audacity to claim the throne of Balagh and the life source of water for his own. To lead a life of pleasure with a want for nothing whilst we live a life of misery and suffering with drought and starvation."

At these words, those around the stones stood, snorted and scraped their sharp claws on the hard ground with their powerful hind legs.

"My brothers, we cannot take Balagh alone and I therefore ask for your help. For this you will be paid in land and a seat at this high gathering when I assume control and become the rightful king of all the lands."

The two kings from the far north looked at each other whilst the third, although not a king, sat motionless and continued to stare. After a small pause they all stood, their thick padded and scarred paws turned outwards as a clear sign of allegiance. Clais stood and reached out to a small metal bar that had been sitting in the fire to his right. Fur and skin of his dead father wrapped thick around the distal handle.

On pulling it clear, the leaping fingers of red, orange and yellow brightened to add the final bit of heat that lit the distorted orange tip that formed a jagged unrecognisable shape. Blont stepped forward and escorted the first of the Kings the short distance to a cleared smooth rock that lay directly in front of Clais. As he approached the warm glow of the rod, the heat radiating from it could be felt from some considerable distance away. The first of the kings who had travelled from the rising pinnacles to the far northwest, knelt, placed his right paw across his chest and braced himself for the impending pain of the branding to his right shoulder. A stench of singed fur was quickly followed by that of burning skin. A gentle rustling breeze whispered through the trees as the high canopies closed in as if discussing the unfolding events. A small cry of pain whimpered from the mouth as the metal rod was removed, pulling and tugging as it gripped the skin as if alive and enjoying the pain it had inflicted. When it was lowered back to the fire, the licking fingers of flame grabbed it in anticipation, rushing to reheat its friend in hungered excitement at being drawn again.

The same ritual was applied to the second King, again when the hot poker was placed on the shoulder, an immediate whimper accompanied the forceful pressure applied.

Finally, Shroud moved forward and knelt, not as a King but a defector from Broadback's troop. Now a close friend of Clais, he had proved himself as a powerful ally with an in-depth knowledge of Balagh's defences and Tronta's likely strategic tactics in defence of Balagh. He knelt, awaiting to be branded to complete the allegiance to the Clais Troop.

Blont stood close as the heated rod was again raised from the fire. Suddenly, with a trailing light through the dark night sky, the metal bar swung hard and fast, impacting heavily on the side of the bowed head. Shroud fell to his side with a crash, the impact both devastating and accurate.

A large, ragged wound opened in Shroud's flesh. Blood flowed freely and ran from his snout to his mouth and out of his ear. His powerful hind legs rendered temporarily paralysed, scratched aggressively at the dry dirt in a vain attempt to regain his feet.

Clais quickly moved to stand over him, having returned the weapon to the fire. He stood menacing, staring down with his teeth glowing white in his retracted gnarled smile. Blont moved to his brother's side and stared down in silence, both breathing deeply.

"You, Shroud,' Clais said in a menacing tone, "alerted Broadback of our plans for an attack."

Shocked, Shroud stared up at Clais with panic firmly set in his widened eyes. Thoughts of escape ebbed away at the realisation of his impending fate.

The initial frantic scramble in his legs faded until they became motionless. "You cannot win," he said between defiant coughs, as he struggled to breath, and spat blood from his drooling broken mouth. "Broadback and his troop will kill you and your brothers as they killed your father. Your evil cannot and must not rule this land."

At these words of defiance, Clais reached back for the metal rod. His paw missed the protected handle on his blind sweep. The smell of his burning flesh filled the air. With unflinching eyes and fixed stare, he waved the orange glow high in the dark sky. The contrast in colour was like the hot sun had cut a sweeping slash to the dark canvas, pulled it open and was peeping through.

Clais' face broke into a contorted smile. The bubbled, rubbery scar now fully retracted and re-coiled over his yellowed teeth. Each visible tooth was long, wide and pointed. The front hung down over his bottom jaw and embedded into the thick scar tissue that only served to highlight size. "Broadback knows nothing. What you have told him is a lie, false information fed to you to weaken Broadback's defence and I thank you for that. Having already sent his troop to the opening to the north where they will stand alone and confused, Broadback will be alone when we attack from the east. We will enter Balagh unchallenged as Tronta stands alone two days from the slaughter that will take place. Broadback and his remaining loyalists will be overwhelmed. All he knows to be good, will be lost. I will not kill him instantly. I wish him to suffer like I have," he growled. "I wish him to feel the loss and anger I have." Clais paused for effect. "He will watch as all those who have believed his lies - die. Young and old. We will rid the land of those loyal to Broadback. Only then will his true anguish start as he will be banished to roam the land alone and blind to the world when I take his other eye for myself."

Coughing and spluttering congealed blood and spit, Shroud braced for what was to come. He turned and stared deep into the dark forest where his eyes fixed on a high rock outcrop. The trees fell silent. Through the pain, he shouted his last stand, determined to not look at his slayer. "Broadback, forgive me. If only I had known the true plan."

With lightning speed, the glow that acutely illuminated the scene, disappeared in an instant when the rod was plunged into Shroud's chest. The crackle of breaking bone and whoosh of escaping air followed the powerful blow. A sudden shock and glazed vacancy fell across his eyes. His head lolled to one side - his tongue fell loose. At its tip, thick blood trickled its length before dripping to the ground, sticky warm and wet.

Clais continued to stare at the motionless body with pleasure. The shadows of the fires danced with a fevered vigour. The hot poker still plunged deep inside the ribcage of the cooling corpse.

The two kings stared at the ground, not willing to engage with the eyes that were rigidly fixed on them as Clais' brothers sat close.

Clais leant forward, his pink charred paw pulled the poker loose, lifting the body off the ground slightly as he shook the poker free. The deep internal tissues had moulded and gripped tight to the foreign intruder and held on in defiance. The weight of the carcass finally gripped by gravity, eventually won the argument. Standing tall, Clais hopped back to the high central rock. Without thought, he cast aside the poker, which was dark and black at one end, red and reflecting wet at the other. The fire welcomed its return with crackles, sparks and hisses as the wet blood met the heat and sent up a metallic stench.

Blont returned to his stone and moved to face his brother, who now sat staring at those who filled the stones before him. The acrid metallic pong of burnt blood and flesh lay thick in the air. Some of those with bowed heads, coughed as the stench settled in the back of their throats.

"The time to rise is coming. Broadback is building his defences and will send Tronta and the troop North. How ready are you to take arms?"

His brother spoke first. "We have massed our best, trained them hard and have thirty-two ready and awaiting your command."

The Kings also spoke in turns, standing to deliver their message and then settling back in silence. They informed Clais and his brothers that they had twenty-seven and thirty-eight ready to join and battle.

Clais remained motionless, his deep-set eyes dark, unreadable. "We shall meet here again at the next full moon due on the setting of the thirteenth sun, when we will head south. We will travel the land together and attack on the rising of the seventeenth sun when the ground is cool and the land in Balagh is dark."

At this, the two kings stood and bowed before disappearing into the darkness of the trees from where they had emerged. Clais turned and headed into the shadows of the large stone and vanished. Blont waited until the meeting had finished before he, too, moved off into the darkness of the trees and vanished from sight. The stones now silent, the fire's intensity waned.

As if permission had been given by their absence, three dingoes crept out from the cover of the trees under the watchful eye of the moon. They approached the still warm corpse, eyes darting, ears high and ready to run should they suddenly be threatened. They were not disturbed. As they approached the body, they descended on the area of least resistance, the large open wound to the chest. With teeth bared, tongues drooling, they began to devour the warm meat.

Sadness and Light

High on an outcrop of rock in clear view of the unfolding events, some distance into the forest amongst the now hushed trees, crouched a small kangaroo, Hale. With ears retracted back, wet nose, body shaking and tears running down either side of her narrow snout, she sat gasping for breath. Now turned from the scene, she stared into the dark tree canopy, eyes wide and her breath short and sharp. The moon had not penetrated the thick undergrowth to expose the intruder. Her presence hadn't been noticed throughout the meeting by those at the stones. She turned again to look down on the now empty site, barring the three dingoes who ate feverishly. She prolonged her final look, remembering her father as he was, not as he now lay. Her dear father had been loving, caring, passionate and a believer in life, love and loyalty. His final words still rang loud. She turned, took in a deep breath with closed eyes and hopped off in a Southerly direction. Within a few hops, the darkness had engulfed her as quickly as if she had fallen down a deep dark hole.

Clearing the trees on the furthest side of the forest, she raced across a large expanse of open ground to another area of dense grass and short prickly bush. She stopped, breathing heavy but conscious to ensure her breaths were quiet and invisible in the cold night air. She sat low, hidden amongst the scrub. Turning on her tail, she focused on the point from where she had emerged. There was no movement or noise from the distant tree line but she waited to ensure she was not being followed.

The only ones who were aware of her fleeting movements were a kookaburra family of five. They peered down. Each huddled close, all with broad, short, powerful beaks and large eyes. Each stared with interest from a high leafless branch of the low dense tree with wide spanning canopy under which Hale now crouched. The family's silhouette was sharp against the moon's cloudless light and was outlined on the flat, sparse, sandy rock.

Hale was thankful the birds did not burst into riotous song. It was as if they knew the importance of her mission for the free land for all. Their silence remained unified, undoubtedly aware it would raise interest in the guards who patrolled the camp on the other side of the shadowed belt of eucalypts.

"Stay calm, Hale," she said to herself, before moving off again with urgency in a southerly direction, keen to make as much distance as she could before the sun rose, when meaningful travel would become hard and dangerous. As she skipped between rocks, her thoughts returned to Balagh. A memory surged when she played with her best friend Filor, with whom she had bonded before moving away with her father when she was two. She remembered protesting at the move from her family and friends but now in his death, understood the importance with pride, the mission for which he had kept secret. She reasoned his silence was to protect her from an almost certain death – hers - at the paws of Clais. She had left Balagh at such a young age and pondered if this was a part of the overall deception in an attempt to show Clais the seriousness of his betrayal towards Broadback. Leaving such a comfortable life for an unknown and uncertain future and acceptance by Clais, with a baby whom he claimed to have found next to a dead mother whilst travelling north, seemed almost unthinkable. In her reflection, it showed what a master of deception her father must have been. It was now clear the betrayal was one of information dissemination, his sole and primary intention.

On the death of Krage, she now knew her father had been asked to infiltrate the north raiders and alert Broadback of their plans with regards to the inevitable retribution. Her thoughts returned to her father who now lay dead at the hands of Clais. His final message, his final words to her, "Broadback, forgive me, if only I had known the true plan." She deciphered it to mean Broadback must know the truth. His words echoed loud in her mind at the same time she sensed a grip in her paw as if he had squeezed it with his final words. Her thoughts returned to the present and as if suddenly charged by a bolt of lightning, she fled.

King Of The Boab

Thulo stood next to his brother Gribe, under the large Boab. The shade provided by the large branches that spanned from the bottle-shaped trunk, gave welcome relief from the sun that was at its highest point. The Boab had a shiny hard silver exterior, both smooth and cool to touch. Its position next to the billabong provided a continuous supply of water to its deep reaching roots. The Boab's bloated lower half indicated in its girth that it had over the years, overindulged and was surely close to bursting.

Thulo stood watching with interest as a spiral of ants formed an ever-changing line from the tree's base to the first of its large spanning branches. He marvelled at the unity in their file, streams ascending and descending, each driven, motivated and all-consumed in their loyalty to the nest's success and an allegiance to the solitary queen. He glanced at his brother who quickly looked away and pretended to engage in the conversation with the others who had congregated.

Looking at his brother Gribe, he still had feeling of loyalty and love. Although he was now considerably taller than his brother Gribe held a formidable presence. He was thickset, with a wide hip, which made him powerful in stance and surprisingly nimble in turning and twisting. This was demonstrated in his mock fights with Tronta while preparing the troops for

the impending battle. His top half was, however, disproportionate to his lower half. His shoulders were narrow and his arms thin and there was notably some loose flesh that sat around his hips. His fur was thick and bristly and stretched in some areas where his underlying skin had been exposed to the sun. His face was wide with a short snout and etched with a continual tension. However, despite his appearance Thulo knew he would be a formidable foe in combat and one he would himself not like to face one on one in a fight to the death.

There was a sudden unified shuffle in those who had gathered. Each vied with a nudge to stay in the shade of the trees leaves and trunks as the sun continued along its arching path. Thulo looked away once the manoeuvres had finished. His lazy stare fell on the wall of red rock that stood high and imposing above them. On the other side of this large rock face, meandered a path that had protected him on numerous occasions during their games of ghosting. It had also been the location where he ran through memories of his father, mother and Filor and his heart skipped a beat at this thought.

As he stared up at the red rock, he moved slightly to his left to avoid a single beam of light that shone straight and true through a gap in the tree's foliage. Adjusting his eyes, he noticed something different: an odd anomaly in the defined sharp lines of rock which sat against the backdrop of blue sky. He noted a subtle change in its colour and shape. Straining, he made out what he thought to be the features of his sister's and Filor's inquisitive faces, both of whom were wide-eyed in their silent stares. He blinked, coating his eyes with refreshing cooling liquid as the warm drying wind passed through the gully and worked to dry them. In a split second of a solitary blink, they were gone. He continued to stare and after some considerable time spent scanning the rock's edge, they didn't reappear. An internal argument raged between his eyes and brain with an agreement that the day's heat and wind had played their game between the flicking leaves of the tree and his wandering thoughts.

Thulo turned and stared across the billabong. Three large pink-legged birds waded through the water's edge. Each stopped abruptly as if the world around them had ceased spinning. Their long, pointed beaks hovered motionless over the water's surface before they suddenly plunged, each pulling out a wriggling fish. With a flick of their heads, the fish were thrown into the air, spinning silver and light before being deftly caught and swallowed whole. The area in which they stood now cleared of any further food source, the birds continued their slow dance across the billabong.

From the large deep red cave, Broadback crossed the short distance to the Boab, accompanied on his left by Tronta who looked as serious as ever, his disabled arm swinging rhythmically with each hop. The boomers moved to face them, Gribe pushing through to the front.

Thulo suspected his brother's action was purposeful to obscure his direct eye line to Broadback and Tronta. However, being physically taller than most he had a full view of what was about to unfold.

Broadback came to a slow stop some feet from the mob, eyeing each in turn before he spoke. Thulo again noted how big his father was, which was considerably taller and broader than all those he faced. The intensity of the sole blue eye was a standout within his broad defined features. His scar was a reminder of the reality of war and the injuries they may in turn have to endure.

Broadback took a deep breath, "Thank you," he said in his deep humble voice. "Thank you for standing by me as your King.' He paused and swallowed. 'But of far greater importance is the loyalty to the land we all call home and the love we share for each other. As you know, Clais has amassed a large troop of some seventy boomers and is headed towards the opening. I have been informed that an attack is planned and they intend to enter Balagh through the northern entrance on the rising of the seventeenth sun. This information comes to me from Shroud and his allies. I trust him implicitly and therefore deem the information provided to be true and accurate."

Thulo noticed the look of anguish in his father's face as he spoke.

Tronta remained silent but a rage was notable in his eyes behind his furrowed brow. Thulo knew that Tronta thrived on conflict as if he wished for war and chaos, opposed to living a life of calm and tranquillity.

Broadback continued, "I ask that you travel the days to the opening and build our defences and ready yourselves for battle. What I am about to ask is more than I hoped I would ever have to do as your King. We are being forced to act and act we will, to protect and maintain our way of life and the future of Balagh." He took a deep breath, "There will be losses to life.' Pausing, he swallowed deeply. "I will gladly lay down mine if that is what is asked and in turn, in protecting our land, for you to lay down yours if so needed."

At this, the group stood a little taller, silent and focused, all unflinching. On finishing, Broadback went round the troop and individually thanked them for the mission and sacrifice they were about to make. He advised he would see them all on the rising of the new sun before they departed. He turned and looked directly at Thulo for a split second before moving off with Tronta in silence. Gribe did not turn to face his brother before joining them both on their return to the cave.

Cough and Splutter

Bob lent over the central consul of the troop carrier, where he picked a chequered blanket off the floor and neatly draped it over the two large rifles lying across the length of the rear seats. Sitting back, he put on his seatbelt, the audible click halting abruptly, clearly annoyed at the time taken to end its frustration.

Bob reached up and pulled an old map from the sun visor strap. He opened the folded paper filled with lines and colour before he followed one particular line with the tip of his finger to the track on which they now sat and tapped it twice.

George put the glinting bottle of water back into its plastic holder, the fluid swishing high to low and side-to-side. He wiped his chin with the back of his faded blue shirt before placing the car into low gear and releasing the handbrake. After an initial jerk, they moved off. The water again splashed around excitedly within its confined clear plastic wall.

They headed down a narrow winding track. The dry spindly bushes that obscured their view, scraped along the car in a physical protest at the presence of the large, loud, smelly intruder.

"Thanks for coming with me, Son. I have always wanted to travel this route like your grandad did many years ago. I can't believe he travelled this exact track. But today we are

going to make a detour, make our own adventure for your kids to follow one day."

Bob looked at his dad with a wry smile and could see from the side profile, the excitement in his eyes. He noted the similarity in his father's facial features to those of his now deceased and beloved grandad. The deep crevices that ran from the corner of his eyes flowed across his face, each telling a story of the ages. Smiling his dad's glasses, which sat on his cheeks, lifted off the bridge of his nose slightly, which always made Bob smile.

"Look on the map," said George in an excited voice. "Look for the outcrop of rocks with a gap between the ridges. It's not named, but that's where we are heading, my boy."

Bob glanced down at the map. His finger slid on and off the faded lines as he concentrated its tip, made all the more difficult with the rocking and rolling of the car on the unsealed track.

"Off to the right, Bob, there it is," his father said, glancing between the track and the rolling map. 'Three days and we will be there."

Bob's finger left the track and moved across a wide river before landing on a large, high circular rock outcrop. The coloured map showed the cliff's gradient in narrowed lines of light and dark browns. As his finger followed the rocky sweep it ended at the break between the two high rocky walls. Within these walls the vast landscape was flooded red.

'Got it," Bob said, circling the location with a thick black pen. "Three days." Looking up, he ducked instinctively when a large green branch ran across the top of the car with a loud scrape, angry sharp fingers grabbing through the open window which he wound up quickly with the wobbly chromed handle.

Light and Shade

Hale sipped water from a small rock pool that had formed over thousands of years between two large rocks. The ravine in which she now stood, provided a much cooler temperature from the open land from where she had just travelled. The sheer walls of reds and oranges cast a continuous shadow at its base with sunlight only touching the very highest points in the vivid blue cloudless sky. She lapped the water gently, her curled tongue holding the cool liquid. Her ears faced forward, her nose twitching, attentive to any would be threat.

On having her fill, she lifted her head to the vertical wall of red rock and noticed the green bushes and small trees that protruded out of the crevices. Each shrub was thick at the base before it bent and headed skywards in the hope of absorbing the sun's limited rays of life as it passed over the ravine. There was a noticeable water-stained jagged line that ran down from high to the ravine floor. The trees and bushes followed this descending stain where water ran during the rains, providing nutrients and life like an artery through a body. The water stain ended its long journey through a moss filter which overhung the small pool in front of which Hale stood.

Continuing her gaze upwards, she sensed a strange disorientation. The crisp blue sky was contained by a neat line of red rock. This gave an illusion she was looking at a winding river with the optical sense that she was in fact looking down from a great height upon its slow meander. Looking forward and then back in an attempt to reorientate her senses, she noticed her tracks lay clear in the sand and small stone. In the open, the wind would have removed her existence and direction of travel. But the wind did not have the same influence in this place. As such, Hale hopped off and headed quietly towards the first bend, taking care to stop and assess for any danger before she continued her journey through the ravine.

The dingo stood at the entrance to the large high-walled ravine. His fur absorbed the heat from the glaring sun that hung in the sky above. He did not flinch, but silently panted, whilst he stared and sniffed the air. Two other dingoes had their heads bowed, sniffing widely but moving collectively inwards as if in a descending funnel of steep sand to a narrow opening. In this case, the entrance or exit, depending on the direction of travel, was the ravine.

"No tracks could be found," they said in unison to their pack leader, Arole, who did not answer but his stare remained as if he could see through the rock to the distant exit point. His wet nose flared as he absorbed a sudden smell in the air.

"She has passed through the entrance," he said in a hissy growl. Without further words he moved off quickly into the shadows, followed closely by the others who licked their lips feverishly.

Goodbye For Now

Thulo stood alone, staring across the billabong. Swirls in the water created from the daily life cycle kept his attention; fish chasing insects, birds chasing fish, each churning the water that mirrored his thoughts, which were swirling and slow. The sun glinted and swayed across the water's rippling surface. He blinked rapidly, hoping to burn the images of the beauty of the billabong into his memory; images he would surely call upon over the coming days. Filor approached and stood next to him in silence. Thulo was barely aware of her presence as he desperately tried to remember every single smell and sound with his eyes closed tight.

"It's almost time," Filor whispered, understanding the importance of the moment all too keenly.

Thulo opened his eyes. Staring up at him from the water's reflecting surface was Filor's beautiful face and wide caring eyes. He absorbed her features in awe. She was reading his thoughts as they stood in silence, before they moved instinctively and held each other's paws. He turned to face her and in doing so, she stood in the shadow cast by his large frame. Thulo felt the early morning sun prickling on his back as if being prodded by a large hot finger affronted at not being able to hear their conversation.

"I am going to miss you so very much, Filor," Thulo said, his voice soft and wavering. "Please don't worry, I will be fine and when I return, I look forward to spending more time with you." He paused. "To get to know you better. Look after Whisper and my family, especially Whisper, who will need her best friend at this time."

Filor gripped his paw tighter. "I fear there is something not quite right, I don't know what, but it just feels wrong. I beg you to be aware of what's happening around you. Don't do anything foolish." Her voice broke on the final words.

Thulo leant forward and they gripped each other in a tight embrace. Thulo noticed how her head turned and lay across his chest perfectly. He gently placed his head on top of hers and felt her pounding heart. But her eyes were far away, searching the horizon and the adventure that lay in wait.

Call To Arms

"Stop mooning around, Thulo, and get ready." The words were loud with a harsh undertone. The call came from the direction of the shadows of the large cave where some fifty boomers now stood. Gribe stood slightly distant from the troop. He stood with an aura of annoyance in his stare and agitation in his fidgeting stance.

Thulo broke the embrace with Filor, turned and headed to stand with his brother. He didn't dare look back as he forced his thoughts to focus on the task that now stood before him.

As Thulo moved through the troop, the majority were quietly discussing the coming days. There was a sense of energy and excitement in the air. It was palpable to the point he could almost taste it. His thoughts were filled with questions and scenarios that were a myriad of bright swirling colours, none of which made any clear sense. Any clarity of thought was blocked by the constant banging noise that only he could hear in the confines of his head.

Whilst waiting for his father and Tronta to address the troop, he was drawn to the dancing shadows on the wall. The sun's peaking rays were low enough to shine under the defences of the cave's entrance, illuminating all those insides. The orange rays silhouetted each of the boomer's shadows which moved and jumped and pulsed on the uneven, undulating rock like some grotesque insect. Lost in the mesmerising movement, Thulo did not notice the ambient noise dissipate, and the cave fell into silence. When he turned, he realised he was the only one left facing the depths of the cave, his thoughts lost in the faces of his forefathers. He quickly moved to join the rest of the troop. His father and Tronta stood at the entrance with stern faces.

With a deep breath, Broadback spoke. "The time has come to defend our home, our honour to those who have gone before, and for those who are yet to come. You will be faced with anger and hatred, but I ask you not to yield, to never bow down." His voice deepened. "Know this, you fight with your brothers and if you fall, travel in peace and know you will always be remembered and you will always have a home in Balagh." He fell silent again, his electric blue eye meeting each and every one of those who looked upon him.

Those who faced him, straightened to their fullest height and firmed their stance, a collective pride pulsing through them. Individually and collectively, they understood the enormity of their undertaking.

Thulo had never seen his father act this way before - hard, merciless, frightening. Standing at the entrance, he seemed to fill the space as if he had grown tenfold. His blue eye now turned dark and narrowed in his frown. His words were meaningful, trusted and spoken by a king, for whom they would willingly give their lives.

Hopping forward and now in touching distance, the troop also moved closer and filled the gaps to a tight pack, wisping steam rising from them.

"I have arranged for kings Trigor and Grolt from the south and west, along with their finest warriors to meet you in three suns' and moons' time.

Tronta moved forward and spoke. The flow between himself and Broadback seamless as he maintained momentum in their unifying message. "We leave today to fortify and prepare for their attack."

Thulo could hear the clear excitement in Tronta's voice. He thought, unlike himself, there would be little preparation required for the harsh travel and brutality of war for him.

"We leave when the light passes over the old tree and the rising of the moon, so we travel in its cooling light." On these final words Broadback bowed his head to each, gripped each of their shoulders, offered words of encouragement and gratitude. On patting the last on the back, both Broadback and Tronta turned and headed down the small bank and out to the water's edge where they stood and drank alone. The silence broke upon their departure with a fevered inaudible hum of pitch and depth.

Thulo left the troop, having made his way through the bustle, blinking as his eyes left the shadowed cave into the light. He felt suddenly lost in the outside space which appeared unrecognizable although this had been his place of birth and the only place he had ever lived. This was his home, where he had grown and played over the last four years. He passed faces of bucks who were evidently talking with him. Mouths moved although silent to him. He hopped blindly, drifting as if a ball of tangled tumbleweed being blown aimlessly in each and every direction, wind depending.

On reaching his quiet place, he stared unseeing. As his brain re-engaged, he took in the scene around him and had no short-term memory of the short journey he had taken to get there. After a few minutes, his vision reconnected with his brain and a warming peace settled over him at the sight of the distant hills. He closed his eyes and took a deep breath. He focused as if standing in the cold water of the billabong. His breathing slowed and the billabong's beauty flooded his mind's eye. The peace and calm were all consuming in the smells and sounds he brought to life. He was momentarily joined by the scurrying lizard with flicking tongue and broad wide smiling head. They sat together in silent wonderment, each seeming to recognise the expansive beauty upon which they both looked in the early morning sun.

Exit and Entry

Hale approached the final bend in the narrow ravine path. She peered around cautiously. Before moving off, she took the time to watch and listen, using her keen sense of smell and sight. With no threat evident, she hopped out into the wide-open expanse and what would be for her, her exit point. Instinctively, she searched the vast open land that lay before her for any obvious threat before turning to study the sky to assess the weather directly above from where she was currently protected. The high walls both ended in a ragged, pointed ledge both of which pointed south. The safe narrow path she had followed through the ravine had made her feel safe and loved and was somehow strangely familiar. Having now ended; it was as if the ravine was a loving mother who was encouraging her newly born to leave her tight confines to commence their first few breaths of a new life's journey.

On continuing her skywards gaze, she was struck by two large swaying trees to both the left and right sides at the very end of the jagged rocky outcrop. Their trunks were short but wide and the foliage on both was flame orange, both in full bloom. Both trees appeared to be stretching their limbs across the gap as if straining for their very first touch. Being trees, she thought the anticipation would be almost unbearable. Slow building growth over many moons and suns, she was sure that when the time came it would be worth the wait, like her father's warm embrace was to her.

Hale took her final cool drink from the crystal-clear pool as grey clouds blanketed the sky above. She drank slowly, allowing her stomach to fill, aware that drinking quickly would be a false economy to her thirst. She raised her head, and now hydrated, felt a renewed energy pulse through her. The sky over the distant pinnacles quickly darkened. There was a strengthening wind that was firm enough to flatten the fur on her chest. It was as if a hand was reluctant to let her leave the safe confines of the ravine at this new impending threat and was gently guiding her back in.

The wind suddenly hit her with forceful gusts. The distant dark sky was mottled with varying shades of grey. Hale knew this to be rain from her years living on this land. A small outcrop of high pinnacles lay some distance away across a large open expanse of arid land. She focused on this being the first goal in her continued journey to Balagh. The highest point of the outcrop was already disappearing into a grey shimmer. Instinctively, she headed off with little hesitation, picking up speed as she hopped down the slight embankment and headed directly for the pinnacles that lay ahead. Reaching their base, she climbed cautiously, following an invisible illuminated trail that only her eyes could see. There was a considerable amount of scrambling due to the irregular and erratic rock displacement. The climb was steep, unrelenting and fraught with danger both seen and unseen. Her sharp black claws gripped and splayed on the rock as she finally pulled herself to the top. She stood momentarily breathless at the exertion and peered down onto a canopy of sporadic trees and thick bush that filled the void between her and the next peaked outcrop of rock.

The trees swayed and moved, giving the appearance she could, with good balance and faith, step out and hop across the gap as if grass on an open plain. However, she knew the reality to be much different. A steep dangerous descent, loss of visibility and direction with increased danger from lurking predators and natural pitfalls. The wind was now strong and constant with no abate. She subconsciously braced, lowering herself onto her small but powerful legs and used her thick tail as an additional anchor of stability.

With a final glance back, she wondered if the winds had allowed the swaying branches on the cliff top trees to finally meet. The gap remained, but not through lack of extended effort by the swaying branches. However, something else caught her eye at the base of the exit to the ravine. Through the darkened sky and falling rain, stood three motionless figures. Their individuality of light colour stood in clear contrast to the rocks that surrounded their tightly knit grouping. She squinted, then focused her keen vision on the figures, which to her surprise, suddenly moved collectively in her direction.

Her heart jolted as if hit by a bolt of lightning as the rumbling in the storm clouds boomed overhead. Beating drums pounded in her ears, which drowned out the wind, rain and thunder that rumbled all around her. Although cold, she suddenly felt hot and prickly as her senses heightened tenfold, the small hairs in her dense fur now standing erect. All her senses said move, her individual twitch fibres coiled like tight springs, as adrenalin coursed through her, 'stealth walkers," she said with a gasp.

Hale watched as the three mottled shapes moved low and sleek, with purpose and speed. She turned, her pupils now large, each eagerly grasping what meagre light was available to help her plan her next move. Instinctively, she paused to steady herself to meet a particularly strong gust of wind and punch of rain.

"Plan, focus, believe and adapt," she said out aloud. With these words she was momentarily taken to a memory of standing next to her father. In her vision, she was about to embark on a race around the billabong with her brothers who had completed the circuit and now stood watching and laughing at having always won this challenge. Her father had whispered, "Plan, focus, believe and adapt."

With her father's words resounding in her ears as if carrying him with her, she stood stationary, visualising her route. She finished in record time and felt the embrace he gave her and the exhilaration in her heart. Suddenly, and like a friendly forceful slap to her face, a gust of wind made her stoop and firm her stance.

The reality of the situation quickly returned and her stomach lurched. The three Stealth Walkers had already covered half the distance to where she now stood. She also recognized in horror that their distinctive fur colours and movements to be the same that had fed from her father's corpse.

With this, she leapt forward, the route she was taking alight as if the brightest of stars had been plucked from a clear night's sky and placed either side of a path she now followed. She moved quickly, sliding on small stones and grabbing onto rocks to slow the risk of a fall and possible break to a bone, which would surely result in the end of her life. She reached the bottom of the steep slope and disappeared into the thick trees and scrub as if a cold dark hand had scooped her up and closed around her in a tight protective fist.

Into The Unknown

Thulo took his first hop. The sand on his paws felt different - harder, hotter and somehow unwelcome. Over the last four years he had hopped every inch, touched every rock and crevice of his home, until they each became a familiar friend with a particular purpose. But this was not Balagh. He eyed across the now wider and much bigger expanse of undulating colour. The foreboding view may well have been another world. Suddenly overwhelmed, for what he had taken for granted as a secondary friend now appeared alien and a threat. His third and fourth hop was like moving through an open door to a large endless room. Thankfully, some familiarity remained as he noticed the faces of his family and friends who stood by his side. Each stood silent and focused, each stared and concentrated on the task that lay ahead and wondered if they had the same thoughts as him.

Tronta stood proud at the head of the troop. The wide shadow he cast gave the impression it had cloaked them in a protective veil as each waited for his command. He turned to face them. "Time to move, my friends and family. Let's kill these marauders." with a wry smile.

Thulo eyed him and reflected on those words. "Kill these marauders."

Filor popped instantly into his vision, her eyes smiling, their quiet walks together, her laugh loud and sweet. His thoughts turned to the billabong with the gentle water lapping upon his paws. The frog that smiled at him before kicking off as it interrupted his first thought of embracing Filor. The lizard who was the consummate spectator with its flicking tongue and razor-sharp toothed grin. The shared moments with his mother, her kind words of encouragement intertwined into the games they played.

Whisper appeared in his visions, shoving him over in the billabong. His younger sister, Lyrea, acting out his performance having nearly drowned and the subsequent act of trying to remove the fast-drying mud from his fur. He would surely miss life if it ended. For the first time, as he stood gazing out into the unknown, he realised how much he loved life and what the future might have looked like for him.

He was suddenly brought back to the present when Tronta spoke again. "We head for the outcrop to the right." He pointed with his good arm, his left hanging lifeless and twisted. The injury was sustained during the initial attack from the North Raiders many, many full moons ago. Tronta had fought ferociously with a fire in his heart, tenacious and merciless in his killing.

The debilitating injury was sustained in the final throes of the battle between Broadback and Krage. With Broadback's back turned, one of Krage's allies, metres from landing a potentially deadly strike, was narrowly deflected by a lunging Tronta, his left arm deflecting the strike. The impact of momentum and deceleration snapped the shaft instantly whilst further tearing the tendons and ligaments in his shoulder resulting in it swinging loose, like an old clock pendulum. The assailant fell to the ground with the impact of Tronta's assault. In turning to gain his paws, the assailant's neck was broken by a heavy and deliberate stomp. Rage and satisfaction had burned in Tronta's eyes, any pain unregistered, his duty done, his friend and King defended.

In the far-off distance and with a keen eye, they could just make out a small outcrop of rock that jutted out on an otherwise smooth canopy of silver sand. As they followed his direction, they all knew this was where King Delanor, Broadback's father, had lost his life in that cave. He was bitten by an unseen yellow eye that sat coiled and ready to strike as King Delanor sat close whilst telling a story of a previous battle. For all this was a sacred place.

"There we will find shade and water and that is where we will rest until tomorrow," said Tronta. He gave them a final look of defiant determination before he turned and moved off, every hop powerful and purposeful.

New Horizons

On a high outcrop stood Filor. She cut a solitary figure, staring out as she watched the group move off unseen. She felt pride and love. Her thoughts swelled and stomach squirmed, her breathing quick, unregulated, sharp. She gripped the rock in front of her for support, the urge to call out Thulo's name almost overwhelming. Her mouth opened and with a deep breath taken she slowly closed it again with a silent exhale. Her voice silenced, overruled by her primary and more powerful thought that Thulo, her kind dreamer, now needed to focus. She knew that any distraction by her calling out to him would only be a selfish distraction. She knew he needed to be fully focused whilst travelling unknown lands and facing an impending battle with the north raiders.

Suddenly there was a scuffle and shuffle to her rear. The narrowed path obscured by rock could not silence the noise of movement. Whisper suddenly appeared, exuding her usual joyous energy and excitement. She stopped with a skid.

"Right, are you ready?" she asked with a lisp, her voice high with each word spoken quickly as if in a close race and bouncing on the spot.

Filor turned away from the now distant party, now a unified shimmering mottled shape, definition stolen as the distance grew. Whisper was of a similar height and stature; the defining difference was the colour of their fur and eyes. Filor's bright white chest almost glowed, a defined shield surrounded by browns and golds, Whisper's green eyes were ablaze with excitement.

"I'm ready," Filor said.

North To South

Clais stood staring out over a rocky outcrop to the distant land flanked by a large group of boomers who stood in silence to his rear. The two kings either side of him. The same two kings who had witnessed the murder of the traitor Shroud, who had infiltrated the Clais troop at the gathering of the circle just three suns before. The murder without judge or jury was a vicious and merciless act. The infiltrator was found to be a close ally of Broadback and had been providing the details of Clais' planned attack to allies and friends of Broadback. However, Clais had known that the spoken loyalty to himself was indeed a lie. Before murdering him, Clais told Shroud of the terrible pain Broadback and his kin would face by his surprise attack from the east.

The kings had joined Clais on the promise that they would gain more control of vast pockets of land to the north, northeast and in future battles to the south, east and west. They also welcomed the notoriety of having a designated stone at the Clais 'rocks' and having the ear of the future king of all lands. They also recognised that for them personally, they would reap the rewards that came with such an elevated status.

The distinct difference of the massed clans was noticeable, namely by their colour and size. The boomers to the northeast had coarse red fur, stood tall, broad in frame and muscular across the shoulder and chest with long powerful snouts. Those to the northwest had a greyer, less coarse fur, slightly shorter but broad with powerful hind legs, shorter snouts and fiery by nature. Both clans presented equally as formidable opponents. Each king had brought their finest and most powerful boomers. The warriors had less to gain than their kings but each promised wealth and most importantly access to unlimited water.

Each stood in their respective troops, both clearly hesitant and untrusting of the other. This mistrust had been interwoven over generations. Each sat and listened to family tales, fathers and grandfathers talking of violent clashes between the two, each seeking land, water and wealth for their own, no matter the cost.

They were on top of a high point with the south passage spanning out before them.

"We continue south; we reach water tomorrow at the distant outcrop beyond the cluster of trees between the two high peaks near the exit of a ravine." Clais spoke in a deep rasping voice, air rattling through the gnarled scar tissue on his lip, spit building and bubbling as the words were formed. He pointed to a distant outcrop of pinnacles that peaked and pointed through darkening skies. The high points were the gatekeepers to the entrance of a ravine which when entered, would take them South. At the highest points of each stood two trees. Even in the darkening skies they were ablaze with orange flowers which swayed in the distant storm of wind, rain and thunder.

Aim and Fire

The wood splintered from the power of the projectile's impact. Half of the remaining wooden board was left spinning in the gentle breeze. The other half landed some three metres away from the old rickety post that stood slanted but defiant. The board had been hastily secured by a solitary rusted wire that now hung freely from the post, weathered but happy to be of some use once again.

"Good shot," George said looking through his binoculars. The distance to the target was just out of reach of the old, scratched lenses of his bent glasses.

"Thanks," replied Bob with a tone of cocky assuredness whilst still staring at the target with a wry smile on his face.

George stretched out his right hand and Bob placed the rifle in the palm, avoiding any contact with the sand which would surely stick to it. His knuckles, however, did touch the sand with its weight. Small grains of gold clung to the thin sheen of sweat that covered his skin. They had decided to only use one of the two rifles to cut down on the cleaning. George referenced this one as the newer rifle: the one Bob had used in previous shoots and therefore was at a considerable advantage.

"Don't worry, Dad, if you miss that's okay, but a good shot never blames his tools."

Before George could respond, Bob added. "Be assured, I will get the kill shot for both of us when the time comes."

George grinned at Bob who continued to stare at the target, chewing a small toothpick which moved rhythmically between his lips.

"Don't you worry about me, Son. I was doing this while you were getting your bum wiped by your mum." Truth be known, George felt a little hotter than normal. His large leather Kookaburra hat absorbed the sweat that was quickly beading as he peered through the telescopic sight. Blinking, he took his final breath which removed the rhythmical motion of the distal end of the barrel and when it fell completely still, he gently squeezed the trigger. With a recoil in his braced shoulder the distant target splintered once more, dust ballooning in a small cloud beyond the target, before being carried away in the breeze.

The spinning wood landed close to Bob's and the other half spun on the wire, one way then the other as the coil wound then un-wound.

"Yes" he cried out in relief before he could control his outburst of emotion.

Bob looked at him and smiled. "Fair play, maybe you will be useful on this trip after all."

Bob placed his hand on top of his dad's. He noticed for the first time his father had changed, he had aged. His skin appeared worn and tired, hanging more than it used too, the lines and wrinkles on his face highlighted in their depth by the fire's dancing light. But, between the wrinkles, his eyes shone bright with love and wisdom. They twinkled with excitement, clearly loving the experience with his son, a cherished memory for both.

"Right," said Bob looking enthusiastically into the pan that sizzled and popped on the fire. "Time to eat." Both leant forward and filled their plates with anticipated excitement.

The Hunted

Hale stood motionless, all her senses working in unison, her calmness her only friend as she strained to hear and smell for any change in her immediate surroundings. The bushes in which she now stood, towered above her, making her decisions, which were literally life or death, all the more terrifying. She estimated she had covered half the distance to the next pinnacle, which once scaled, would be her exit out of this place. She also knew the pursuing stealth walkers were hiding somewhere in the undergrowth and likely closing in.

The rain and wind continued to swirl, which she knew would shield her movements from any unwanted sound. However, within such a confined space between the trees and scrub she would inevitably leave her scent on leaves and branches which would indicate her direction of travel. Plan, focus, believe and adapt, again stabilized and calmed her thinking which was eager to run wildly and blindly. This sequence of words had supported her whenever she was confronted by a problem. On this occasion she chanted them in her head, unlike a few moments ago when she heard herself speak them aloud, which she was prone to do from time to time.

Suddenly she was overcome by an overwhelming sense of calm. The natural desire to bolt, which would have been unfocused and unplanned, faded. More unexpected, the wind momentarily stopped. The rain continued with audible tapping of water falling from high foliage to lower leaf then to the ground. *Tip, tap, tip, tap* at different intervals, pitch and tones depending on the height of the accommodating plant and subsequent distance to the ground.

Hale held her breath, sure her pounding heartbeat could be heard throughout the entire valley in the temporary silence. She placed her paws across her chest in an attempt to somehow muffle the *thud, thud, thud.*

Crack! A small twig broke off to her right, followed by another, *crack*! Surely it was caused by the weight of a paw. Hale hunched over, almost lying flat, breath stifled, completely silent. Straining, she heard distant whispers which seemed to move towards her before moving off and fading away.

As quick as it had ceased, the wind rustled through the leafed foliage. The accompanying rain increased in its tempo as the skies overhead darkened once more. Where Hale had lain just moments before, was now empty. All that remained was flattened grass and leaf. The surrounding foliage swayed briefly in an opposing direction to that of the wind before joining the general sway once more as the damp grey fog swept in.

Hale pushed forward through the wet foliage, her fur now dark and sodden. Suddenly, she stumbled into a small, elevated clearing. At its centre was a large grey craggy rock. On a quick assessment and with all her senses tingling, she noted one side had a graduated and relatively flat platform to an unknown height. As her eyes followed the outline through the fog, she made out a small shelf which offered some considerable height above the canopy from which she had just emerged. She stood stationary and stared as her mind worked feverishly on what to do. The risks were stark. She could forge ahead in the wrong direction and unwittingly come across her pursuers. The alternative was to climb the rock, establish where she was and plan her next focal target and direction to her escape. However, scaling the rock would almost certainly give away her position as she would be exposed and visible to her pursuers.

She stood still, thoughts tumbling. The risks for both were equal and very real. If seen by the stealth walkers they would cover the ground far quicker than she would have time to escape, especially coming down from such a height. She took a deep breath and asked in a whisper. "What do I do, Father? Please help me."

The wind and rain continued unabated.

"Adapt to your situation," he would have said. "Life is not easy, it's full of choices and difficult ones at that. Work through the scenarios then choose the one where you can implement controls and where the risks are considered and weighted. Once you have decided, commit, focus and believe. Stick with the plan unless the variables you can't control change, when you then adapt and plan again."

Hale studied the rock, now focused and committed. She cautiously approached the side that offered her a way up and began to climb.

The Happy Dance

Filor and Whisper reached the bottom of the steep incline in silence, a sense of purpose palpable. They entered the green undergrowth before they dared turn to look up. Both recognised the importance of the mission they were about to embark on. The two large rocks, which were always so imposing, now appeared almost small and insignificant from where they now stood. Filor had never ventured this side of the protective wall that encircled her home. The walls had provided her the security of love and familiarity since her birth three and a half years ago.

And now she was leaving with Whisper for the first – and possibly the last time. Whisper turned to face Filor and could read the hesitancy and worry in her face.

"Are you sure you want to come with me, Filor? There are no guarantees and I have no idea what we may face. We have a long, long way to travel with no idea of where we will get food or water. We have no idea what may wish to do us harm and what challenges and decisions we will face and have to make in battle."

Filor stood face-to-face with Whisper and knew that what they were about to embark on was full of danger, this reiterated by the seriousness in Whisper's words and body language. Strangely it wasn't the unknown that scared Filor, as her thoughts drifted to her family. Filor loved her mother and father and her sisters Kryle and Teney. Teney had sadly passed away at the age of two when she fell off a large rock. The resulting break to her hind leg was an injury which made her sick and one that she ultimately never recovered from. Filor's parents were very loving, equally quiet and very caring, with grounded morals and a sense of duty to their community. Both ever reliable, steady, no surprises, predictable.

The loss of Teney had only heightened their community involvement, no doubt a distraction from their lifelong grief. Kryle was a year older than Filor and very different in almost every way. She was born with an adventurous side, excitable and always on the search for the next challenge which often led her into trouble. However, Kryle settled when she met Lanort. Her focus changed to making plans, which included a family of their own. They had a beautiful daughter and two very active sons and with parenthood came predictability. A platform of steadiness and risk-averse thinking slowly crept into their lives as they worked to curb the excitement of youth within their joeys. They were all settled, living a safe life where each day replicated the last and there was no plan for this to ever change.

"Filor?" Whisper stood close and smiled with a glint in her eyes. With a joint smile and a bracing hug, they turned and headed quickly through the low-lying bushes in the direction of the distant unseen opening which lay some three suns' and moons' travel away.

"We need to follow the outcrop as close as we can as this is our only reference point," said Whisper, referring to the large and formidable wall of rock that ran North. Every hop they took was now uncharted, unknown and exciting. They covered the ground quickly, both conscious that they had a lot of ground to make up if they were to arrive at the dawn of the battle and join the Tronta troop. Whisper took the lead and moved into the shadow of the rock face which lay to their left and towered high above them. An impregnable guide that only allowed one direction of travel. Every hop they made would further distance them from a home that offered them the security of familiarity, family and safety.

They stopped after they passed through a clearing and took a glance back from where they had came. Against the backdrop of the night sky, the two large stones they had passed through had merged and melted from view and sat somewhere in the distant darkness. The rock formation they now followed, stood illuminated by the twinkling stars and moon which shone bright as if supporting them on their quest. As they stared up, an occasional streaking light whizzed across the sky before disappearing without a sound. The trail of bright light momentarily burned into the darkness.

Filor's thoughts drifted as they moved quietly through the scrub. What was Thulo doing and thinking at this very moment and what would he say if he knew she was on the other side of the red rock wall in stealthy pursuit? Filor's thoughts then drifted to how similar her and Thulo were. Not the loudest amongst the troop, both enjoying their own company but also just being together. She liked how considerate and thoughtful he was. But she also knew and had seen, when warranted, an unseen strength of conviction and an undeniable sense of what was right and wrong at the foundation of his very core.

Filor's thoughts turned to herself and how she would have been considered by her family and friends as safe, a non-risk taker, and reliable. But here she was, travelling across an unknown land, which was dark and imposing and shared no real understanding of the dangers that lurked and what they were going to face at their journey's end. Her inner voice said with pride, "Look at you," as if surprised. "Facing your fears, aren't YOU the brave one, aren't YOU the adventurous one." As the voice fell silent, a large grin spread across her face. She had confided in her sister, Kryle what she intended to do. She had entrusted her to tell her parents and to support them through the worry her action was likely to cause. She wouldn't allow her thoughts to linger too much on the anguish and stress her parents would feel, so she blocked their faces from entering her thoughts. But her love for Thulo and her inner spirit to do something meaningful was, ultimately, greater than any stress this journey would cause her family. She reasoned that if she returned, she would explain her actions and face their questions when she saw them again.

"Stop," said Whisper in a quiet voice as she crouched low and moved silently behind a large rock.

"What is it, what have you seen?" asked Filor. She peered around and saw nothing but silhouetted trees and bushes in the moonlight.

"Over there." Whisper pointed into the distance which was on the other side of the rock.

Filor moved cautiously and quietly to where Whisper stooped and stared with a frown. As her brain worked to adjust her eyes to her surroundings, a task not helped on this occasion by a sole wandering cloud that muffled the moon's light. Her eyes then fell upon a faint orange and yellow flicker dancing merrily on the distant plain, silhouetted on the other side of the river by the night sky.

They sat and watched, fully focused and mesmerised. All of a sudden, the light vanished into darkness which once again consumed all they could see. They continued to stare thinking they may have lost sight of the orange and yellow dance. Maybe mesmerised, their gaze had drifted from its brightly coloured hypnotic twinkle. After a few minutes they looked at each other. "What was it?" said Filor, "and what's that smell?" she added as she put her nose in the air to sniff the gentle breeze rifling through spindly bushes.

"I don't know but we need to keep moving, it just doesn't feel right." They turned and headed off into the shadows.

Full Belly's and Happy Hearts

That was bloody beautiful," said Bob.

"You can't beat bacon, beans and sausage," said George as he washed and dried his plate. He moved to his tent, clasped the small metal tag and unzipped it. He sat inside the entrance and took off his boots and hung them up, ever fearful the night-time wildlife might find a deep dark boot a suitable and kind offering of a new home. The tent swallowed him whole as he threw himself inside. The gaping mouth was sealed by the zip as Bob was engulfed by the brightly coloured devourer of humans.

"Goodnight, Son, love you."

"Goodnight, dad. It's been a good day, love you too." George replied from the beast's bowls. The fire now extinguished, lay silent. The smoke silently rose as if the souls of the deceased embers meandered upwards towards a smoky heaven. To their East, the moon highlighted the high rock wall which they intended to follow north at dawn.

Hide and Seek

Hale stood next to the rock that towered above her. Wary, she took a few hops away from the rock to assess and plan her next move, the plan phase in her four-pronged strategy. Now fully visible and looking up, the rock was at least six times her height. The levelled platform on top could not be seen from the base. Its defined outline appeared to end, from what she could see, in a point that faced the direction she planned to travel. She hopped back into the rock's safety once again and breathed deeply.

The wind and rain whistled around the immovable mass which shielded her like a welcome friend. Its huge back turned and stooped over her as if protecting her from the wind's onslaught. Looking left and right, the rain obscured her vision to less than twelve hops. The wind whistled louder in a high-pitched scream as if shouting in annoyance at the rock's efforts to protect the weak. Fully committed to her plan, she gritted her teeth. The comfort and protection offered was in reality only putting her at more risk by her inactivity. She turned and moved to her left. Upon leaving the protection of the barricade, she was hit by a gusting punch which greeted her as if in hiding and waiting for her to show herself. The whistle turned to screech as if calling for reinforcements having found its illusive prey.

Crouched low in a firm stance, she moved around to face the wall which towered up into the darkness. She studied the line she would navigate, small cracks and crevices providing holding points to place her short sharp claws. She was acutely aware she now stood in the open and not only visible to the wind but to the Stealth Walkers. She was in no doubt that somewhere out there, they continued their hunt. At this jolting thought, she jumped. Her short, outstretched arms found small crevices whilst her back legs drove hard, propelling her upwards. With a scramble and her father shouting in her ear, she pulled herself up and onto the platform. Immediately she crouched and moulded herself into the rock's cold dark shape and breathed heavily.

Her fur was now dark and knotted but mirrored the colours on which she now lay. Camouflaged to her surroundings, she focused on slowing her breaths to a calm, rhythmical cycle. She hugged the cold, hard rock as if a friend. Her internal sense of risk worked hard to override her planning senses and protested loudly about what her physical body was about to do. Hale raised her head, craned her neck to search out and up across the landscape to the peak of rocks which would provide her an exit from her immediate danger. The rain and wind continued with unrelenting fury. Hale squinted and lowered her eyes to follow the line across the scrub to where she would commence her climb. The peak she planned to scale stood high, dark and shapeless under the cloud of rain and wind. With occasional breaks in the elements, she was afforded the briefest of glimpses of what lay ahead and around her. She blinked quickly, a subconscious reaction to the wind in her face. Each gust contorted, to obscure and confuse her view of distance and undulation. Suddenly there was a rumble followed by a loud and powerful *crack* and for the briefest of moments an illuminating light lifted the darkness in the land around her.

In that split second, information flooded her every synapse. She counted several trees that lay in a straight line between the rock and the base of the climb. The distance to the climb on these briefest of glimpses was shorter than she thought. She estimated she had covered well over half the distance from her entry point before stumbling into the opening and the rock upon which she now lay.

Before darkness fell and to her horror, she clearly saw the Stealth Walkers standing to the left and right of a large rock which stood imposing at the base of her intended climb, she estimated to be some sixty hops away. One of the Stealth Walkers stood like herself, elevated on top of the rock, looking back into the flatlands. She quickly dropped herself low, contorting her body to the rock's shape. The sky once again turned dark as the whistle of the wind tunelessly sung all around her. Hale stared in the opposite direction hoping that somehow if she could not see them then they could not see her. The cold of the rock and small pools of water filled her left ear, splashes from heavy droplets caused her to blink and close her left eye which lay in a small puddle of water.

'Move,' she said quietly to the adapt phase in her trusted strategy, now the situation had changed. She arched her head upwards and slowly around to the right. Her fur brushed tight against the cold wet rock in the 180-degree turn. Staring, she waited for the next light to strike as the rumbling continued overhead.

As she stared into the darkness, the lightning came unannounced, followed by a loud crack and rumble. She focused all of her concentrated effort on the rock to where the Stealth Walkers stood. All other peripheral information blurred and became unimportant in her focused stare. To her horror the rock on which the Stealth Walkers had been, was now empty. The bushes at the base of the rock vigorously swayed in the wind. Their exaggerated movement gave her the impression they were alerting her in its frantic wave, to the danger she was now in. Her risk senses fired loud with pops and whizzes before darkness fell once again and a loud rumbling roar filled the air.

Bad, Loud and Sad

Thulo was at the rear of the group, those around him silent as they moved through the night. The silver sand was highlighted by the vast clear cool night which arched overhead. The deep, endless black was filled with thousands of twinkling lights, all of which were dwarfed by the large bright central one which hung suspended and bright.

Tronta continued to keep the pace high, aiming to reach the point of the shadowed overhang and the reprieve of water before the sun rose. Thulo noted how each and every hop Tronta made was forceful, unbothered by stone, barbed plant or heat when the sun was high. His injured shoulder became noticeably more drooped as the supporting ligaments tired.

As they hopped, they passed weird looking objects that Thulo and many of the group had never seen before. They were hard, awkward in their angles with differing colours and strong smells. Each twisted and half covered in sand, the landscapes effort to hide these most awful of imperfections. At one of the objects and noting the interest of the troop, Tronta stopped and stood next to one of the objects and waited for the group to congregate. Thulo noticed that Gribe, who was previously at the rear of the troop, had worked his way through and now stood side-by-side with Tronta and in turn looked stern and important - King-like.

"This," began Tronta, "belongs to the tall walkers." They use them to move around by sitting inside them and it carries them very quickly."

Those who gathered looked at each other - horrified.

"But sometimes they stop, don't ask me why and these big shapes get left."

Confused, they all looked at each other and continued to stare with thick frowns.

Tronta went on. "Tall walkers are dangerous, they can kill without even being close or even being seen," which instantly caused a further deepening in their frowns and an increase in pitch and shuffling within the troop. "However," he continued, "they have not been seen on this land for many, many moons, not since I was small, and Thulo's grandfather was king."

Gribe instantly shot a look at Thulo with an intensity as if looking through him. Thulo studied the weird object again while Tronta continued with his description. Gribe turned to listen and Thulo was thankful for the reprieve.

Tronta hit the object with a rock, the result was a strange clanging noise, his attempt to show the beast was dead. Tronta's final parting words were not to worry, the aim was to stay focused on the battle that lay ahead. Tall Walkers were not to be a distraction.

They collectively turned to hop once again towards the base of the large wall of rock which was silhouetted silvery red. Although high and solid, Thulo tried to imagine the world beyond it, which spread out in all directions and as far as the eye could see. Thulo had never ventured to the other side of the range, but it was one he had looked out upon when he sat with the lizard in his now, not so secret hiding place. There had never been a need to leave the security of Balagh in his four years of life as it provided all of his worldly needs. What lay beyond was unknown, unsafe. As Thulo drifted towards the back of the group, he noticed in the still sky beyond the high wall, a mysterious white whispering cloud that slowly rose vertically and high into the dark sky before disappearing. Thulo looked across the troop but none of the others seemed to have noticed this strange out of place cloud. They had their heads bowed in silence, some talking about what Tronta had told them about the Tall Walkers and the danger they presented.

Suddenly there was a horrible scream. A terrifying sound that left none within the troop in any doubt that one of their own was in immense and unimaginable pain. The sound was like nothing Thulo had ever heard before. A cold wave swept through him and as it did, it grabbed and pinched his skin, his fur hair rising to stand erect. The group reacted with a start, each stopping with a jolt. A sudden cloud of hot air quickly plumbed from their quickened breaths which hung motionless in the cold night sky.

Tronta burst through the group, seeking the source and direction of the scream which continued and echoed around the walls that lay but a short distance away. Lying on the ground, and kicking wildly, lay Elimir. The resulting dust rose to a short height, sitting suspended in the dense cold air. Surrounding his thrashes, the scene was one of complete confusion. Multiple visual and physical stimuli flooded and dampened the brains of those who stood nearby, helpless and confused. Each tried to understand the scene upon which they looked. Most of the troop quickly and silently moved to secure their immediate surroundings as if they were about to be attacked. They had practised this move multiple times at the Boab, circling it and facing outwards. Their positioning was one of being staggered, one slightly forward of the other to cover gaps to the left and right in the event one of their comrades was to fall.

Thulo was close to the source of the scream. However, the direction was hard to pinpoint as it echoed around the rocks. Suddenly, Tronta knocked him to one side as he charged through. Thulo, on gathering his senses, looked where Tronta now stood motionless some twenty hops away, his back turned so he faced the scene which remained obscured. The scraping of claw on hard rock, and whimpers could still be heard. Thulo moved to join Tronta's side. On doing so, he could not help but stare as he tried to understand the horror of colour and movement which filled his vision as if he were looking through a kaleidoscope. The scene was horrific. His heart quickened and pounded even louder, his ears bolt upright, his nose twitched with no control.

He was looking down on three limbs which flayed. Each trying independently to gain traction on the dirt and rock which offered no support with each forceful strike. The fourth limb lay independent and still. It sat enclosed in a clasp of teeth which had locked tightly, tissue and bone exposed, blood dripping thick and sticky at the point of severance. The colour of the culprit was the same as the Tall Walker object they had previously seen and touched earlier that evening. Dark red, flaking and as dead as the limb it now gripped.

Gribe burst into the scene and without hesitation, kicked the trap which overturned awkwardly but still held firm to its prize. The noise upon his forceful impact was one of a clunks, clangs and rattles as metal struck upon metal with differing tones at the violent strike. The clamped jaws were attached to a thick low-lying tree previously hidden by a scrub plant. Under the moonlight, the lighter flesh of the tree stood illuminated where the chain removed gnarled bark in a circular ring.

Gribe moved to stand over his friend whose movements were now noticeably less, blood covering a large area upon which he lay. Small red sticky balls of sand lay in the deep scratch marks created from the initial panicked thrashing which had now subsided. Gribe stood and stared, desperate to think what he could do for his fallen friend. Elimir's right leg was missing below his knee joint. Blood continued to drip, albeit slowly, from the open gnarled wound. The large pool of blood below the stump reflected the stars in its shiny thick glassed reflection.

Thulo watched at how quickly the reflection dulled as the fluid, which was no longer oxygen rich, also died and was absorbed by the welcoming sand. The ebbing reflection mirrored the reality of Elimir's last gasps of life.

Tronta moved forward to meet Elimir's wide frightened eyes, lowering himself and placing a firm paw on his comrade's bloodied chest. All panic suddenly dissipated as Elimir fixed his stare on Tronta and raised his paw to grip his friends.

'I am sorry,' he whispered and coughed. "I wanted to be with you in battle." He paused between quiet gasps and blinks. "May the Kings be with you and provide safe passage on your return to Balagh, victorious."

Tronta paused and swallowed. He firmed his grip. "We will be victorious and when I see you again. I will tell you of our victory. Travel safe and be happy in knowing that you have done your duty."

Elimir stared skywards and with a final breath and a faint smile, all pain left his face. He closed his eyes, his grip loosened and his paw slowly slid off his chest to lie by his side.

Night Scream

Whisper and Filor stopped dead. Both turned to face each other in the darkness, eyes wide and gripping each other's paws.

"What was that? Was it a scream?" asked Filor.

"I don't know," said Whisper in a quiet voice.

"Do you think it was one of the troops?" asked Filor.

Whisper noted the concern that was evident in Filor's voice. "I really don't know."

There was a long pause before Filor spoke. "Do you remember when my sister broke her leg when she was young?" She paused. "The scream sounded so familiar." She trailed off with a worried frown. This had resulted in her eventual death.

Trying to inject positivity in her tone, Whisper said, "I am certain that, if it did come from the troop, Thulo will be fine. You know what he's like; he wouldn't put himself in trouble. He avoids trouble unless confronted, so don't worry." She spoke in a tone that was so matter of fact any other consideration would be out of the question.

"Yeah, you're right.," said Filor, with a brighter smile. "There are loads of things out here at night, any one of which could have made such a noise and there is no way we would have caught up with the troop already."

Whisper agreed. The Tronta troop had left some considerable time before them which added another layer of positivity. "You know what Tronta is like, he will drive them hard, so my guess is it was something completely different and nothing for us to worry about. Especially since we are on this side of such a huge, insurmountable wall of rock."

At this, Filor smiled and they continued through the thick scrub. They talked as they moved, recounting stories of each other's families, games they played. They relived yet again, the infamous Billabong Incident. As Whisper finished the story with high-pitched excitement, they both fell to the ground in laughter, recounting Thulo's face covered in mud and wide-eyed, frantically wafting his paws around at the cloud of humming flies that had descended upon his face. As they slowly regulated their breaths and with hoarse throats, they heard a rumbling noise; deep, loud, continuous and powerful and not too far away.

They both sat up at the same time and remained silent, angry for the noise they had made in their laughter, which could have put them in danger. They headed down a small single track, evidently in the right direction as the noise became louder and even more fierce.

"Come on," said Whisper as they rounded the base of the trees and crouched. When they exited, they were met with a burst of rain.

Hell and High Water

Clais moved forward, the rumble almost deafening as the river below swirled, coughed and roared while it grabbed and ripped up everything within its destructive path. The bank upon which he stood was loose. The moisture and mud pushed between his paws under his heavy weight. As he passed by, parts of the bank tumbled into the rapidly moving water where it was quickly swallowed. The river roared dark at its core, spraying white froth like spittle in fevered excitement. There was no natural path down to the water's edge, the steepness upon which he looked, clearly too risky to descend. To reach Balagh, the river, at some point, needed to be crossed. However, this juncture was too dangerous with its height and swirl.

'Let's move,' Clais roared and pointed for those who stood behind. His voice was too hard to hear at the very rear of the strung-out line.

The Southerly direction where Clais was now headed, was flanked to the left by a line of trees that stood swaying on a high rocky sparse outcrop. The troop that followed did so without question. Ahead of Clais, moved five large boomers, each hugging the trees when they rounded sections within the undulating path. Clais followed the same line as those who moved ahead of him, his features expressionless despite the rain that lashed hard and directly into his face. Suddenly, one of the trees whose roots were now exposed by the river's torrent, gave way under the weight of the lead boomer who clung to it in shock. The four boomers directly behind him turned and hopped backwards as the dirt around the base of the tree shifted as a large solitary muddy clump. The roots could now be seen and were heard snapping like arteries and veins, as if a heart had been torn from a chest. Now unshackled from the earth, the tree fell forward and slid down the bank.

With all his power, the boomer jumped from the clump of earth, reaching the bank where his claws dug deep into the soil and clasped a solitary root which remained firm. His eyes wide, terror clearly etched onto his face as his powerful back legs dug into the soft bank which offered no firm support.

Clais quickly hopped forward, past the other boomers who scrambled onto the security of firmer ground. Clais stood looking down into the eyes of the boomer who pleaded for help. Stooping down without hesitation, he reached to his fullest length with a wide-open paw. His thick forearm pulsed with blood, arteries running proud over tendons which moved individually in response to his knuckled pawed movements. His muscular arm and back, now soaked by the rain, only further defined his muscular features to those who looked on to his rear. The boomer loosened his grip on the soil and thrust his paw upwards into that of Clais at his instruction. With his back turned to the troop, Clais closed his paw around the wrist of his comrade. The roar of the river some thirty feet below, sounded louder than ever as if hungry and begging for fresh meat. Clais' eyes narrowed, dark and glinting in his deep furrow as he gripped tight on the joint, claws penetrating the skin. Red oozed from the puncture points before being absorbed and diluted by the rain. The resulting screams of pain were muffled by the noise.

Those who stood some considerable distance back, mistook the inaudible sound as a result of his predicament. Clais stared, unbothered by the rain and weight pulling on his shoulder. Water ran down his features, funnelling off his scarred ugly lip to the tip of his nose. The water and phlegm streamed onto the face full of fear that peered up at him. His gnarled lip curled; teeth exposed in a grimaced attempt to pull; the effort visible in his shudder.

The boomer now hung from the bank, swinging helplessly with desperate hope in his widened eyes and mouthed voiceless pleas.

The bucks who stood watching, glanced at each other, shocked at the strength being shown by their leader as his body shook with the strain. The ledge was too narrow for them to help. Clais raised his head and shoulders with effort before he dropped forward dramatically. His shoulders lurched forward to stare directly into his comrade's eyes, whose pupils were wide and scared.

With a smile, he whispered as he leant forward. "You are weak, and I cannot have weakness." He momentarily tightened his grip, paused, grinned and let him go. He watched as the boomer fell, arms and legs flailing, eyes terrified and shocked before landing hard in the dark water with a deep splash which swallowed him whole. His rear leg and long tail rolled before disappearing out of sight.

Clais stood still and smiled wide before he turned and fell to the ground breathing heavily. His smile was replaced with a grimness of distress and fatigue. His brothers rushed forward to help their leader although he waved their help away. He slowly stood, swayed and looked across to those who stared at him in awe at the bravery he had shown.

"I couldn't hold him, I tried to save my ..." he paused, "your comrade. A true warrior who will be remembered for his allegiance to our cause."

He stood breathing heavily. "Please bow your heads and remember him."

Following his orders they bowed.

Clais delayed his bow, his gaze taking the time to note their grief as his eyes flashed and his scarred lip twitched. He turned. "We must carry on; we cannot let his death be in vain." He delayed raising his head until he assumed all others had raised theirs and were looking at him with admiration. Five new boomers rushed forward to navigate the narrow ledge as they continued to move south, the rest following in silence. Clais hopped towards the rear of the troop with his face contorted in sadness although his unseen eyes narrowed in a smile.

North and South

Filor and Whisper lay breathless, having witnessed the events from the high bank on the other side of the river. Lying flat, and hidden, they continued to stare as the final boomer gingerly rounded the last bend and disappeared out of view.

"He let him go; he let him go." Filor said, then added "did you see his smile?" in a shocked voice.

"They're heading South," said Whisper as if she had not heard Filor.

"What?" said Filor, turning to face Whisper, "what does that mean?"

"Well, the entrance is north. They are heading south. It doesn't make sense," she said in a quiet voice as if her brain was in deep internal conversation with itself.

"The battle is north," tailing off as their eyes met and in that momentary silent stare it dawned on Filor what Whisper had said.

Filor spoke her thoughts to confirm the silent communication that had passed between them. "They are heading south to attack Balagh directly. They are going to attack when Tronta and the troop are two days away at the entrance to the North. They will kill everyone, my parents, my sister." Her voice rose. "Broadback will be killed, and our troops will not even be aware. They will hold the high ground, and we will lose our home."

Filor rose to her full height slowly and pushed through the low-lying branches which sprang back to their natural position with a sway. The larger bushes on her passing sprayed small beads of glistening water in all directions as if a handful of diamonds had been thrown high into the air. The rain had stopped but the sky remained thick and grey. The small hanging globes of water that domed from the shrubs, magnified and reflected colours of browns and greens which lay within their immediate surrounds.

"We should follow them. We need to head back to Balagh and warn Broadback," said Filor.

Whisper hesitated. "The troops will be two days away and by the time they return, those who remain in Balagh will be dead." She paused in thought. "And they will be exhausted from the trip back and unable to fight." She tailed off to a mumble.

They fell silent while trying to block out the gruesome visions of death and destruction that simultaneously entered their thoughts. The warmth on their back from the now protruding sun's rays were most welcome. The rain and wind from the night before and from the most recent downpour had caused them both to feel cold to their core. They continued to shiver whilst standing in silence, contemplating what they had witnessed and what it meant.

Unwittingly, the cold weather had also dampened their spirits.

"They are going to have to cross the river to get to Balagh at some point. They will likely look for one of two things, either the water level is shallow enough or the width of the river narrow enough or both," said Whisper, still staring blankly.

The cessation of rain and noise of heavy drops on leaf and ground allowed the sounds of life to be heard once more. The buzz of wings, the call of insects and the flight of birds filled the air although the beating drum in their chests did its best to upset the tranquillity. They both stared at the river. Its loud rush of power and speed could be felt through the narrow gully in which it ran. As they looked south, the river widened and fell to a meander as it rounded a bend and continued its journey south. They both knew it passed Balagh, which was one thing they could not change. Whisper looked at Filor and moved to stand in front of her, raising her paws in an open gesture.

Filor placed her cold wet shaking paws into Whisper's and continued to stare at the ground. Silence fell again, Filor's insides squirmed and recoiled in almost resigned recognition and protest of what Whisper was about to say.

"I need to get to the Troop. I need to stop them, send them back before it is too late. I need to get to Tronta. You, Filor, need to let Broadback know so he can hide our family. They will all be murdered if we don't make it back in time."

They slowly raised their heads, and their eyes met. Filor's were glazed. Her body shook, which Whisper knew was not from the rain, but fear of what was being asked of her.

The noise of life fuelled by the rain and glancing sun's rays, became a loud hum of differing pitches and tones as if all belonged to a symphonic orchestra. For Whisper and Filor the only sounds heard were the uncoordinated deep breaths they both shared as they stared at each other.

Whisper's paws tightened around Filor's. "You're stronger than you think," she said, "look at you now, Filor, here on this adventure." Whisper's eyes narrowed to a strong determined stare, her body moved to square up and firmed in her stance. "We are here for a reason. This is our time to show what we can do. This is our moment to be strong, equal, recognized, remembered. We have always wanted to show what we are capable of. Always prayed for this moment to stand and be seen. Not to just follow the expected life, but to truly stand and be measured against all of those who have gone before. We can change our destinies and for those that come after us, Filor. When the stories are told of the great war and how Balagh was saved, they will speak our names in the same sentence as Tronta, Broadback, Thulo and Gribe."

Filor listened in silence, then pulled Whisper into an embrace and held her firm. "I love you, Whisper, you're the bravest, most courageous and loving friend I could ever wish for."

Whisper turned her head slightly and whispered into Filor's ear. "The second bravest."

The High Climb

Hale took a deep breath and moved low and quick across the ground. Under her paw, the dirt was wet and her prints were deep, providing a clear route map on the direction she was heading whilst slowing her down. The first tree, a key primary navigation point of which there were seven to the base of the climb, appeared from the undergrowth. Her travel was silent, conscious not to disturb the base of the bushes through which she passed. Any unnatural movements in their upper canopy would surely be seen by those who hunted her. Raising her head just enough to see over the low-lying foliage, she picked out the second tree and beyond that the third. She again moved off with little rest, reaching the second and third quickly.

The shadow cast by the large rocky outcrop up the steep bank was now fully visible, its face gnarled, pitted and unwelcoming.

"Almost there," she said and sensed her father next to her. He was also focused, committed, their senses electric, heightened to the slightest sound or vibration under paw. She moved off again. The fourth tree sat on a slightly higher bank to that of the third but the fifth and sixth sat rooted higher still. After a few moments and with no obvious sound of any distant voices or abnormal disturbance in her immediate surroundings, she broke cover and moved off. A small clearing only exposed her for a short distance before she would be hidden again.

On reaching the base of the tree, she moved behind it and peered around to search across the lower lying plain. The view was one of complete contrast. The sky was divided by a sharp line. One side rumbled towards her, a darkness of storm and chaos. The other a cloudless deep blue which was being edged south by the aggressor. A light misty fog that blanketed the lower land, had now dissipated as the rain started once more, light taps landing on her snout. She scanned the land around her and was drawn to, for the briefest of moments, an unusual movement in the low-lying bushes which lay some eighty shortened hops down the bank. There it was again. She focused her stare as a small group of clumped bushes moved in the opposite direction to that of the easterly breeze.

Suddenly she turned and hopped without caution. The line she travelled was the shortest route to the base of the steep rocky climb. Small bushes that filled the most direct route were easily navigated by going around or through them with little pace lost. All her senses screamed for her to look behind but this request from somewhere deep within her brain was denied. She knew from her billabong races that any second of delay or loss of focus could, in this terrifying reality, cost her, her life.

Hale burst through the last remaining shrub, which was thick and tall, its height obstructing her view. At its base sat a thick protruding root, which lay hooked, hidden and unseen. As she burst through it, her trailing hind limb, which was long and thin, hooked underneath the thick arch and she fell and spun, landing heavily on sand and rock. Although the physical motion of hopping had stopped, she remained alert to her situation. She jumped up, her vision sharp and focused on where she had just emerged through the thick scrub. Turning, she glanced left and right to the direction she was to travel. Large rocks of varying heights, red in colour, each appearing sharp and wet and potentially slippery under paw, with narrow gaps which would surely slow her down.

She turned again to search back down the steep bank. To her horror the three Stealth Walkers appeared from behind a shrub and paused in the clearing, having not physically seen her. Their heads were bowed, each sniffing frantically, trying to pick up a scent. Unnoticed, she crouched. She was conscious to keep a clear path of vision from her elevated advantage point to those who were actively hunting her, now just seventy hops away. They were moving left to right in large sweeps, trying frantically to find her direction of travel. Thankfully, the soft mud masked her prints amongst many others who used the trail as a natural thoroughfare throughout the year.

The rain, now heavy, filled the newest impressions, masking her scent in the dark sandy brown water. She cautiously peered up the steep bank to plan her final escape. A wide gap between two large rocks invited her in, but what lay beyond them was unknown. Whatever path she decided to take was fraught with risk and unknown dangers. Whatever option she decided on she had no other choice than to expose herself briefly to her pursuers. Time was no longer her friend. Turning back, she watched the stealth walkers methodically work their way forward. All three inched ever closer to her hidden location and the short track to where she now sat crouched and scared. Looking down, she noticed a trail of large red ants marching menacingly around her paws in annoyance, clearly not aware of her predicament. Looking up through the scrub, she saw all three stealth walkers were in a line, their eyes in her direction. She took a deep breath, turned and broke cover.

Rock 'n' Roll

The distant rocky outcrop rose out of the sand like a mole on sunburnt skin. The fire crackled and spat its anger, small sparks wafting into the night sky before being extinguished by the cold fingers of night.

"That's where we are heading tomorrow, Son." George looked out, before taking a swig of the cold amber liquid, the white head visible in the golden-brown bottle. 'Beyond the outcrop we head to the opening and hopefully we will find some roo's."

The distant rock was covered in cloud and rain which could be seen falling like a veiled curtain being drawn. However, where they stood it was still dry. Bob returned with the map and they sat together next to the fire. The hiss of excitement escaped another bottle as the gold cap was removed, and George took another deep swig of the rising liquid. He wiped his mouth and bristling whiskers.

Bob's fingertip followed the lines on the map which travelled across the large open desert expanse. He then moved his fingertip across the old map to a river that meandered North to South. Bob's finger continued North adjacent to the river and landed on the opening that surrounded the inner land and tapped it twice.

George opened the packets of bacon and sausages with the blade of his Leatherman, wiping it briefly on his jeans before placing it back in its leather pouch and snapping it shut with the round brass stud. The rising aroma of sizzling meat wafted quickly into the air as the pan dance started again.

"Hopefully the rain holds off tomorrow when we head to the river and from there North," said Bob.

They fell into silence as they stared at the fire and pan in anticipation. They reclined their chairs with bottles perched high on their chests as they stared up at the vast twinkling night sky. The orange glow was accompanied by sizzles and pops, the only sound that broke the thoughtful night sky's silence.

The Divide

Filor took her first solitary hop South. Looking back, she noted Whisper had already left from where she had stood just moments before, the foliage swaying gently. Filor stood quiet, motionless, the hum that had existed just moments before now fell to a deafening silence. It was as if all the unseen eyes that surrounded her were staring, waiting for her next move. She knew the decision to separate from Whisper was the right one, but now she stood alone for the first time in her entire life. She searched around, oblivious to the noise of the gushing water that sat at the base of the steep bank to her left. The increasing cry of insects and birds to her right and above all now offered audible advice on what she should do next.

Her mind was a jumble of thoughts and actions which needed to be controlled and calmed. Its whirling energy to be harnessed for the positive. She took a deep breath and closed her eyes. The swirl of voice, sound and light began to slow. Suddenly, as the hum fell silent, her inner voice of reason spoke loud and clear through the internal fog. Head south, follow the river, navigate the cliff base and then into Balagh, her mind instructed. It's a little simplistic, her second pessimistic inner voice added. Blanking out both voices, she cleared her mind to allow her rational thoughts to make the decision. The river and land she would travel were uncharted. She would have to pivot on her plan as she went, since she was sure she would come across unforeseen challenges and obstacles along the way. Opening her eyes the light in her immediate location seemed brighter, the sound sharper, the swirl now calm. Without hesitation, she moved off, pushing through the leaves and branches with a new-found sense of purpose and urgency.

On raising her head after protecting her eyes from swaying branches that wished her well in their touch, she emerged into a bright new world. Light and mottled warmth greeted her on a high expansive platform. Blinking, she gazed in awe on a view which spanned out as far as the eye could see in a southerly direction. The expanse upon which she looked was beautiful. A winding gorge with a thick tree line on the left, the bank to the right upon which she stood obstructed by a sharp bend to her right. She was drawn to the patchwork of colour in the leaves of the trees and noted how they swayed gently at differing times as a wind blew up and around the valley. The visible bank down to the river was a dark red as if a slashing wound through the landscape. The water a long way down the bank was loud with an underlying roar. It bubbled a dark brown and splashed white spray as it bounced off protruding rocks. As she refocused, she looked back from where she had emerged. There now stood a wall of tangled colour, as if a closed gate to any thought of retreat. Down to her immediate left the river churned dark and brown, aggressive in its shout and roar. Swirling waves smashed into each other with white froth spraying into the air as if bared teeth and spittle. Beyond the immediate torrent, she followed its flow that had cut through the land over millions of years. In the far-off distance, it was calm with shades of green as it rounded a bend to the right before disappearing out of sight. As she scanned the bank on the opposite side, the troop led by Clais was no longer visible to sight or keen to her smell.

The first obstacle already presented itself. A narrow path she would have to navigate if she intended to move south to Balagh along this trail. Filor knew from playing ghosting, the loose rubble in the bank presented a significant risk. Even with the most cautious of hops, her weight and movement could lead to the embankment giving way and a perilous unavoidable tumble to the murky water below.

She moved off with little option other than to move slow and with caution. One of Filor's primary fears was stumbling across the enemy troop with no protection or place to hide. She was currently exposed and therefore fully visible to prying eyes. If seen, her fear was to become the hunted and having to escape in unknown territory opposed to her current and more favoured position of the hidden hunter. As she pondered the situation, she was comforted by the thought that if she were to be seen there was a river and steep bank to be scaled before any harm could be inflicted.

She travelled with assured footing, each paw placement considered. She tested every placement to avoid any dislodgement of rock which would tumble loudly down the embankment. However, it was a further comfort to know the noise of the river below would mask any falling rock impact. The river below appeared to increase in pitch and tone as she appeared in full sight for the first time. Its anger was evident as if frustrated that she was out of its cold wet reach. As they stared at each other she had the sense the flow silently worked to erode the bank in the hope it would give way and she would tumble unabated into its open welcoming arms.

Now fully focused, she travelled the narrow ledge. After some considerable time, she slowed to a crawl and edged behind a small clump of thick scrub. She snuck forward to its thick base and sat completely hidden. Across the river in a clearing, the Clais troop had stopped and were talking and feeding on a levelled embankment. Filor easily identified who she assumed to be the troop leader. She made this assumption as he was tall in stature, broad and had, from what she could see in his comrade's reactions to him, an air of authority. He also appeared to be battle-hardened and although not clear from her distance, to have some facial scarring. His only company, two large bucks who stood by his side. Both were huge but only just reached his shoulder. Filor also noticed the differences within the troop. The most notable was how the reds and greys stood separate from each other. The divide was stark. To one side, those who were tall, lean and red in colour. The others were smaller but broader and thickset with grey coats. They stood in tight huddles in deep discussion. Each group appeared to be eyeing the other off. Although some considerable distance away the wafting wind carried their odour, which was keen after many days of travel and she grimaced.

Suddenly, out of nowhere, a loud scream came from a branch over her head. With its hood up sat a large black bird with a bright red flash on its wings. Filor stooped until she was flat, her eyes swinging from the bird to the troop. To her horror, all eyes were fixed on her location. The assumed leader now stood at the head of the troop and stared sternly in her direction. A short time later a distant cockatoo called back from a tree on their side of the river. The bulk of the troop turned in the direction of the screeching response, although the scarred leader continued his stare towards her. Filor stared back, scared the sound of her eye lashes meeting would sound like a clap of thunder if she dared to blink.

After what seemed an eternity, her eyes straining, he looked away. There was a discussion and those who had been lying down now stood and collectively moved to congregate before continuing south. Filor bowed her head, placed her forehead on the sand and took a deep breath, blinking rapidly to moisten her dry eyes. When she eyed the cockatoo, it was staring down at her. It gave one final screech before leaving its perch and soared across the river to the distant trees. Filor stood cautiously, not to her full height and continued on in pursuit.

Hold On Tight

Whisper turned her back on her friend, fully understanding the enormity of the task she had bestowed upon her. Now separated, she whispered "Good luck," before refocusing on her commitment to intercept the Tronta troop and return them south to defend Balagh. She immediately took to studying the large rock face that confronted her some 200 hops away. It seemed unassailable from where she stood and as such an immediate obstacle to her desire to travel north. On approaching its base, she peered up, then left and right, scanning the rock and shrubs for any obvious route to its summit.

The wall extended as far as her eyes could see with no clear way around it. The wall stood firm and mottled in reds, browns and oranges. After a lengthy process of internal discussion, she picked out a narrow rocky ledge that appeared from where she stood, to be well used. Although steep in some sections, it appeared to be her only choice. She had to act decisively as any delay would only lead to the Tronta troop travelling ever further north from her current location and the Clais troop ever further south. To get to the rocky outcrop she approached the torrent of water which lay between her and the climb out of the valley. The recent rains had caused the stream to swell and it now gushed its way through the rocks with a considerable speed and force. She stood at what seemed to be its shallowest point. The clear flow at the water's edge dappled small rocks and stones which flickered gold, brown and green. Whisper could not gauge the water's depth at its centre due to the torrent and swirl, but it looked considerably darker towards the middle. Some seventy jumps to her right, the water disappeared and plummeted between a narrow gully to join the river below which Filor now followed south. She hopped down and peered between the two rocks where the water through like a capillary joining a main arterial vessel. The muffled sound suddenly roared in the open air as it bubbled and frothed white with a misty spray.

She returned to the narrowest point. On her final assessment, she figured one leap would not cover the gap. She estimated at best, seven cautious small hops were needed. She was also very aware of the potential risk of injury to a limb which would inevitably end her mission.

"Focus," she said out aloud. "You can do this." On these words she hopped forward, her long rear paw searching to find assured footing in the water. She immediately felt the biting grip of cold and forceful flow which protested by pushing against her thin limb. Now committed, she remained strong and steadfast. She placed her other paw into the water, felt her pads splay uncomfortably to meet the design of the unseen rocks and stones below. Levelling her balance, she took another hop. She fixed her eyes on a small shrub as a point of focal concentration on the distal bank. Placing her paw into the water with another hop, she found the deepest point yet, the water billowing over her hips with a formidable biting force. She was now four steps away from the bank. At its deepest point, she steadied herself and focused her body and mind on the task at hand. All other sounds and distractions fully blocked out.

Without warning, a large, dark, moss-covered log appeared at speed from between a flurry of rocks behind her. Before she had time to react, the log hit her left hip causing her to lose her balance on the hidden stones. Off balance, she fell onto her back. With no assured pawing she was carried towards the steep drop-off. She coughed and spluttered in shock as the coldness of the water hit, but worked to twist around to face her direction of travel. The log bobbled and spun ahead of her as she approached the gap. The distant plain of blue sky indicated the fall was high and one she would not survive. She tried to place her paws on the stream's bed, but she could not reach the bottom. Thrusting with her right leg, she spun to face the cliff to her rear before thrusting her leg again. This thrust turned her to face the skyline once more and it approached at a rapid rate indicating the drop off was only seconds away.

The log spun a full cycle horizontally before lodging itself between the two final rocks. The water continued to cascade both over and under it with increased force. Whisper was only seconds behind. She raised her arms. The forceful impact with the log hit square across her chest which stole her breath. Her long sharp claws penetrated deep into the wood. The change in her equilibrium allowed her upper chest to move over the top of the log and she lay on it breathing erratically. The pendulum motion allowed her powerful hind legs to reach the shallower riverbed which was awash with smaller stones. The water was powerful and cold and seemed determined to claim her as a gift to the mother river below. She glanced to her left and having established a firm footing, gripped the log an arm's length to her left. She slowly worked her numb limbs in unison on the pebbled stones as she edged herself to a large smooth rock which sparkled in the intermittent sun's rays.

On reaching the rock, and although cold, she planned her exit. She focused on a deep-set root of a tree which protruded from the bank. She gathered herself for the final time and although shivering, reached to her fullest extent. Her claws were at a full outstretch, but her palm pads could not grasp the wood but merely scratch them. Shivering, and with exhaustion setting into her core, she loosened her grip on the log and leapt. The shift in weight on the log caused it to jolt sharply. At this, she lunged for the root with her other paw. The log turned 180 degrees and disappeared with a loud splash some distance below. Whisper pushed with her back legs. The root lifeline remained firm as her paw gripped it tight. With a final push, and using all of her remaining strength, she pulled herself onto the bank and turned onto her side gasping and shivering uncontrollably.

Exit Point

Hale entered the gap between the towering rocks and turned quickly. To her horror, the stealth walkers had seen her dash. Time and sound suddenly slowed to a standstill as their eyes met.

A fire in Arole's eyes blazed with an intense ferocity with undeniable need for death and food. He bared his teeth as all three dingoes disappeared into the final undergrowth that ran around the base of the sparse rising slope.

Turning, Hale focused her thoughts on her escape. She hopped into the gap, looked left and right and assessed her best opportunity for escape. She hopped from the sand onto a large central gnarled rock to gain height.

Even under this circumstance in which she found herself, she had the clarity of thought not to leave track marks indicating her direction of travel. To the right the rocks were noticeably higher obscuring her vision of where the exit path might lead. It would also require a significant scramble to get over it. To her left, the path ran horizontal before ascending and disappearing out of sight. Both offered no indication of hazards that may lay beyond. The sky above darkened quickly. The wind came in forceful gusts as if a knuckle punch. The rain that accompanied the wind, threw large droplets which exploded like small grenades with a sharp sting where her fur was thin. On each solitary impact, the droplets tripled into smaller droplets as they changed her colour, tone and temperature and her grip on the rock. Her exit decisions changed as fast as she blinked. The rain and wind worked to further cloud her thoughts as if a spectator in a blood sport. She became acutely aware that her grip and traction were being stolen under the worsening conditions. The voices in her head screamed to act before her choices were taken from her. She leapt right. Her chest hit the rock with force. Her claws instinctively scratched on the semi-wet rock for grip holds. Scrambling, she stood on top of the rock and stooped low before she leapt to the next before dropping to an uneven trail and heading upwards and out of sight.

The stealth walkers skidded into the opening where their prey had stood just moments before. The rain fell heavier and blinded them to her movements. They searched left and right. They lowered and raised their heads to locate a tracking scent. Her visual tracks had now been washed away. Their height was a distinct disadvantage to scramble up the large slippery rocks to the right. Arole stared left before instinctively jumping between a narrow crevice where he covered the ground with long strides before disappearing out of sight. The two remaining stealth walkers stood in the shadow of the rock to their right before leaping left to follow their leader at speed.

Hale kept her eyes focused as she scrambled across the rocks. The top of the climb could be glimpsed through the wafting mist and rain. She estimated the summit to be no more than 100 to 120 hops away and she quickened her pace, not knowing where her pursuers were. The wind whistled down the hillside with the imaginary force of water cascading from a waterfall. The rain created new streams that gathered pace and ran between the rocks. She targeted these streams as she figured the water would follow the path of least resistance and would also hide her tracks if her pursuers had followed the path to the right. The sparse bushes offered few places to grip or a place to hide so she continued to climb. Her escape was entwined with cautioned speed. Each paw placement considered, forceful with conviction and strength.

The rocks that towered above her seemed to rise and grow even more as she climbed ever closer, ever higher.

Halfway to the exit point was a solitary tree which sat rooted in a small hollow. The wind direction suddenly changed from right to left. The rain still pummelled Hale's coat which was now sodden black. For a split second, she thought this change in weather would offer a degree of invisibility if the wind and rain continued to darken the sky. She again broke cover, and with all she could muster, covered the ground low before entering the hollow and crouching where darkness hid her. The hollow muffled the sound that raged overhead as she lay scanning through the rain for any movement. A whirring and whistling wind slowly moved around the horseshoe shape before re-joining the wind that sped by upon its exit.

All of a sudden, through unblinking eyes, three shapes slowly appeared, steady and silent. The ground they covered was being devoured. It was clear from their direction of travel they were targeting the only remaining tree in an otherwise sparse landscape.

Every step they made without action from Hale, was life ending. Her options were limited to one. Break cover, climb the hill and with the greatest of hope, find trees and shrubs on the unseen side where she could lose herself. Having assessed the incline as being less steep than the right, Hale edged to the left side of the hollow, which allowed for maximum speed. There was no time for overthinking the 'what if' other than taking a deep breath and committing herself to climb as quickly as she possibly could.

She kicked forward. The power generated through her back legs sent small stones flying to her rear and ricocheting off rocks lower down the bank. Hale thought she might as well have been pursued by a family of screaming kookaburras for all the noise she made, but there was little choice. She reached the summit quickly, glanced back and winced when she locked eyes with Arole, who was leading the pack some twenty jumps behind.

With all thoughts of self-care forgotten, she reached the top and descended into the unknown with abandon. Through the rain, she blinked quickly, trying to clear her vision. Her breaths were loud, unregulated, panicked and all thoughts of silence abandoned. Her movements became uncontrolled; her panicked brain was fighting its own battle in an attempt to regulate her uncoordinated movements. Suddenly, she tripped, and tumbled to her right, landing heavily on her right shoulder before smashing into a tree which spun her completely around to the left. All the air left her body. With a gasp, she rolled over and over again before crashing through some low-lying scrub. At last, she landed face down in a cold murky puddle. As she lay motionless, a gushing roar filled her ears. At the same time the sun's warming touch quickly prodded through a break in the clouds to ensure she was okay. The rumbling sound faded as another sense, her smell, ignited and took precedence. A large shadow suddenly covered the sun's rays and she slowly turned and looked directly into a pair of savage eyes. Surely this was the end. Her fate would mirror that of her father, but worse, as she would be eaten alive.

As her vision cleared and came into focus, she was suddenly staring into the face, not of Arole but a very large, ugly face. Glinting drool shone over his gnarled lip. A string of phlegm snapped at its midpoint and landed on her chest with a splat. A smile curled across the grotesque mouth.

'Who do we have here?' snarled a deep, dark voice.

Looking down from the high bank stood Arole and his companions. They lay low and silent observing the scene below with keen eyes. The troop was large and Arole knew Clais all too well, having witnessed his rule and murder far to the north. He turned to his friends and said in a low growl. "She is done. He is merciless. There is nothing for us here, we head home." They turned with rumbling stomachs and headed North, assured of the unfolding scene's outcome, Hales death.

Hale and Clais

Four large boomers hopped forward and grabbed Hale roughly, clearly no consideration for any injuries that may have occurred through the fall. On being lifted from the ground, pain shot through her shoulder and left hip which resulted in a significant limp. She was dragged through the dirt and dropped in a small clearing where a large group formed to have a look and a poke at this most unexpected prize. From the shadows, Clais approached the circle slowly. The group broke ranks before filling the gap after he passed through. All eager for the best view of the spectacle that was to unfold.

Hale stared up at the huge, ugly boomer as he approached. A hatred raged in her eyes which did not go unnoticed. A memory of the most vivid and horrific kind was brought into clear focus. The memory of her father's murder raged through her mind. The look on his face, the sound of the impact to his head. The look in his eyes as he searched the forest whilst facing imminent death and still thinking of others. The terrible smell of his burning flesh and worse, the stealth walkers moving in to devour him.

"You look familiar," Clais said with no emotion. "Your face, your eyes - they look familiar to me." He moved forward to take a closer look, staring, eyes narrow as a thick drool landed on her again.

Hale stared back, holding his unblinking inquisitive glare with nothing but loathing which numbed the fear that would normally have coursed through her. He was no more than a few hops away, now leaning forward and taking in her features. He sniffed loudly before closing his eyes and raising his head.

"Yes," he said looking down at her, "you were part of my troop, brought by Shroud when he left Broadback. Yes,

I remember. He said he found you abandoned; your mother killed by the Tall Walkers. Was that true?"

Hale could see the small sensitive cells working to create the memory of recognition. As she stared at him those who looked on, fell silent.

Suddenly, with his eyes remaining closed, he raised to stand to his full formidable height. With a final snort he peered down at her, his eyes wide and knowing. He smiled, drool running from his chin to his chest.

"No," he said, "you are his daughter. He lied to protect you. You're the daughter of the traitor who died at my paw. I can see it in your eyes, so similar now that I can study you and no doubt you have the same rancid blood in you. Untrustworthy, cowardly." He paused. "He had such sad pathetic eyes, defeated, weak, before dying slowly and painfully without even putting up a fight." Clais was now so close his breath could be smelt. It was sickly warm and putrid.

Hale leapt from the ground, her claws spread wide and teeth bared. Any thought of self-preservation gone, all that her father had taught abandoned, the solitary goal to inflict pain no matter the cost.

Clais, as if expecting the attack, sat back on his thick tail and with a casual kick of his back legs hit her square in the chest.

She was no match for his power and size. She left the ground and landed heavily, pain exploding through her sensory network, all-consuming, momentarily blinding. As she gasped for breath, panic surged for she was quickly crowded by those who had looked on in silence. Staring eyes surrounded her. Voices whispered about what should happen next. All touched and prodded with interest and malice. Strangely, she was not overwhelmed by the seriousness of her predicament, but the pungent smell of dirty fur and bad breath that surrounded her. She tried to stand, pushing herself up with her left paw. Her father's bravery coursed through her. The fuel to push beyond the pain, to stand tall, proud, defiant in the face of adversity and what seemed an almost certain death.

Fear abated. Instead, a warm shield built from within her core, strengthened with every beat of her heart which pounded strong in her chest. With an indestructible armour and undeterred by the close faces, murmurs and hot breath, she pushed through and limped towards Clais whilst cradling her arm.

Clais did not move. He took a deep breath, his chest rose before he exhaled through his scarred tissue, spittle forming to a bubbled froth. Just three short hops away she stopped. He stared down upon her. She barely reached his midriff, but she held his stare, undaunted, unmoved.

The surrounding troop fell silent in anticipation of what Clais' choice of fate would be. The two boomers who flanked his side, hopped forward and roughly grabbed Hale by the arms, paying no attention to the whimper of pain she tried extremely hard to hide. Clais' eyes burned with a deep fire.

"Coward. You can't do it yourself can you?" she said.

Clais smiled. "Time to join your father, give him my best." The two boomers dragged her into the large opening of grass. The rain had started again but was misty fine as the sun shone down. The troop shuffling behind stopped in the shade of the trees.

A jutting point stood before them, the banks to the left and right having fallen away over years of erosion and heavy rain fall. The boomers let her go and hung back by some three hops, although they continued to shuffle forward. Although they did not speak, she felt their menace as she faced them. She could almost taste it. Hale had little option but turned and hopped slowly forwards, the width in which she hopped, narrowing. She peered around and out across to the other side of the river. In doing so, she felt the height of the embankment and could now hear the roar of the monster below, bubbling with anticipation of a fresh meal. She raised her head as the end of her life was just moments away.

A distant rainbow arced overhead. Its colours were bright, crisp and defined with a sharp intensity of which she had never seen before. As she lowered her head, the surrounding sounds and smells were more alive than ever before. It was as if she was being serenaded before the final curtain fell. Closing her eyes for the final time, she took a deep calming breath. Opening her eyes, she found herself staring directly into a different pair of eyes framed within a gentle face hidden within a bush on the other side of the river. She had no idea how she picked them out as they were amongst leaves, but they were large, kind and welcoming. Shocked, she blinked and when her eyes opened again, the face within the bush had gone. She reasoned this was some distant memory but one she could not recall. Somewhere in her subconscious she thought she recognised the face but just could not place a name. She now stood at the very tip with nowhere to go.

The water below was deep and dark. Each dip and trough presented like a gaping mouth, each hoping to be the one that swallowed the offered meal, like young chicks in a high nest. She turned and straightened. The two boomers now stood some six hops away. Clais and the remainder of the troop stood in the darkness of the trees. They stared at each other, and she did her best to hold his stare in a final stand of defiance.

Hale's senses were incredibly alive. The sensation of wind ruffled her fur. The smell of wet soil and budding flowers filled her nose. The sounds of birds singing in the distant winds, the scurrying of insects on the ground below and the laughter of the billabong filled her ears. She had experienced all life had to offer. Love, laughter and friendship. She would join her father and family soon, many of whom she had never met. She was moments away from living a new life of endless warm sun, food, water, games and peace where all lived in harmony. As she shuffled towards the edge, the fear of the river dulled as the angry roar became muffled, almost welcoming. The warmth of the sun on her back for the very last time was incredible.

The boomer's head swam into her view. It grew larger as it approached, then dissolved. A cloud of pink and red mist formed a plume momentarily caught in time and space before being carried off in the breeze.

As if forcibly slapped, she watched as the boomer's head was thrown backwards with incredible force. For a split second, he stood stationary before falling backwards with his back legs upright and twitching. The impact on the second boomer was as forceful as the first. His attempt to retreat into the shade was in vain as he was thrown forward, rolled and twisted to face Clais, his mouth moving in rapid gasps before his tongue fell to lie still and wet.

Clais showed little emotion as he stared into the dilated pupils. He hopped forward, stopped at the very edge of the tree's shadow as the sun disappeared behind building clouds. He stared at the fallen before turning to stare at Hale. His jaw muscles clenched. His chest rose high.

Hale recognized the risk of standing on her own in the open. Although she did not know what had just happened, she figured she had to act quickly as she studied the corpses and then Clais. She turned, her paws on the edge of the crumbling bank. Her weight rocked back and forth. She eyed the water for a split second before taking an almighty leap. She landed hard, before being engulfed and disappearing out of site. Clais stood motionless as if he had been sculpted out of rock. The only movement was his lip which twitched in pleasure.

Kill Shot

"Good shot, Dad," said Bob. George smacked his hand in a high five then gripped it tight. "But I have never seen that before, in all my years hunting, I have never seen a kangaroo just fall off a ledge, almost intentional."

"Don't worry about it," said Bob, "we've made our first successful shot of the journey." Standing from the high bank.

"Next time can we pick some targets on the same side, the thought of Kangaroo steak is making my mouth water," said George.

As they bickered about the distance and which kill had been more impressive, they spied the biggest boomer they had ever seen emerge from the tree line. His coat was dark brown, almost black, wide stance, tall, broad and staring directly at them. They had secured their rifles against a small tree fifteen feet away to protect them from the rain. The muzzles were settled in the natural divide of the trunk which was the perfect height and size for them both. Bob quickly moved towards the tree, leaving George staring. George raised his glasses high on his furrowed brow and replaced them with his binoculars that hung from his neck. His fingers worked to adjust the central dial to clear focus, which brought him face-to-face with the boomer who stood motionless, staring at him. George gently adjusted the magnifier to take in his features; wide, taut with the deepest eyes in a thick browed skull. The most noticeable feature was the gnarled purple lip that cushioned large, pointed teeth. As he zoomed out with a twist on the scope's dial, he was speechless on how broad and muscular this boomer was. Although it must have been some 180ft away, he felt strangely uneasy at the boomer's motionless stance and unblinking stare.

Bob arrived by his side, all attempts for stealth clearly abandoned in the rush. He now stood in full view before he laid down and fiddled with his scope. As he did so, George said, "Put it away, it's too late." He watched the boomer turn and disappear into the tree line which was dark and thick. "That," he fell silent for a long period, "was the biggest boomer I have ever seen. He had to be seven feet tall."

Bob scanned the tree line himself, but the darkness of the canopy engulfed all as the clouds once again rolled in overhead.

Deep Breath and Hold

Hale rolled and tumbled, over and over again through the dark cold water. The occasional brief visit for air, grabbed in a frantic breath as she worked to stop the spinning which was taking her one way and then another. She grabbed blindly, each closed grasp holding nothing but the coldness of liquid which dispersed and ejected playfully through her paws. Through sealed lids, the darkness of depth, and light of the sky above shone through her thin skin as she spun and twisted. The independent hands of the water's torrent prodded, gripped, grabbed and pinched at her. Her mind became increasingly unfocused and desperate as the noise and speed of which she spun was at the total mercy of her cold captor. Suddenly, as she was forced into a deeper spin, her head hit a rock which was large and sharply angled. Her breath expelled from her in plume of crystal bubbles.

The cold fingers of water prised her mouth open further and in her unheard scream, death rushed in. She opened her eyes in panicked confusion to see a wafting cloud of red. This was quickly diluted and replaced by a muddy brown swirl. Strangely, the panic that had consumed her now dissipated. Her thoughts became strangely warm and foggy, almost friendly. Death's warm words flooded her canals with the promise of what awaited her if she were to simply stop fighting and in its whispers of kindness, she listened.

In the flooding tranquillity she suddenly felt pain in her back, high up in her neck. She felt betrayal from death which promised warmth, love and for the pain to stop. This new pain pierced, gripped, strong and was unrelenting. The accepted darkness was replaced with light as her head broke free of the water's clutch. She was being pulled onto cold rocks which stabbed through her bones and muscle in their unevenness.

She coughed in rasps in her eagerness for air. Within each bark, strains of blood mixed with thick congealed sputum, sprayed from her nose and mouth. Her eyes blinked rapidly as light and darkness brought into focus a watery shadow. Her ears ignited to life on the shake of her head to make sense of the noises that surrounded her. The overwhelming sound was one of concerted huffing and puffing which made sense when combined with the frantic grabs. The pain doubled as a further grab and pinch of claw travelled from her shoulder to her now firing cells in her hip.

"Help me, help me," came the voice filled with tones of urgency and exacerbation.

Hale opened her eyes to the sound of the voice. She peered into an upside-down face with wide caring eyes, open mouth and loud rasping breath.

"Hale, come on, we don't have time to waste, they will be here soon."

"Filor, is that you?" She coughed again, the last of the water shot out, blood slowed to a trickle from her nose.

"Yes, come on."

Hale responded by turning to place her paws on the cold rock upon which she lay. The water lapped at her tail with tiny pointed white fingers trying to pull her back in. A grand prize once owned, now being stolen in broad daylight.

With a final cough she stood and met the eyes of Filor. Memories full of warmth flooded her as she was transported back to Balagh. Memories of chasing each other, hiding, talking, laughing. Hale considered Filor to be her best friend and secretly, her feelings extended beyond simple friendship. Before she had chance to express her true feelings, she was taken north by her father. However, her feelings for Filor never changed. In fact they only grew stronger in their separation as she reminisced on their times together. She hoped and prayed for the day when she would have the opportunity to tell her how she felt and could only dream that Filor felt the same way.

Without warning Hale embraced Filor. Her body jolted, her muscles suddenly warm as her blood bubbled and her stomach squirmed. She raised her arms and placed her paws on either cheek of Filor's face and gently pulled her head from the embrace. Staring into Filor's eyes, there was such an overwhelming, pent-up emotion, she moved to kiss her.

Filor quickly looked away and after a momentary pause, Hale coughed, more in embarrassment. They both laughed and embraced again. After a lengthy silence they felt their friendship ignite and flow between them as if they had never been apart.

"Where have you come from.," asked Filor, voice urgent.

"Far to the north," said Hale. "I have been travelling for a full moon and sun. Clais is travelling south, not to the north and will attack to the east.," she paused, taking a full breath.

"I know.," said Filor. Whisper and I were heading North to join the battle when we came across the Clais troop heading South on the other side of the river."

"Where's Whisper now?' With a sense of dread she automatically looked back to the river.

"She is heading north to stop the Tronta troop and have them return to Balagh. My task, which I now guess is our task, is to return to Balagh and warn Broadback. He needs as much time as we can afford him so he can prepare, defend and hide the old, young and weak," said Filor with mirrored urgency. "Where's your dad?" she asked, remembering him playing with her in the billabong and telling tales at night when the young sat gripped with excitement under the great tree next to the billabong.

Hale swallowed deeply, her eyes filling with moisture without warning as she looked at the ground and sagged.

Filor immediately grasped what her response meant. She moved forward and held her friend in a firm, protective embrace. The adrenalin which had driven Hale for the last two days had finally run empty. Filor braced to support Hale's weight as she sagged and sobbed uncontrollably into Filor's chest.

Exit Point North

Whisper stood, having gathered her breath. She peered out over the ridge where the river disappeared into the distance before it meandered off to the right. She wondered where her friend was on her journey as rain fell in the distance. All Whisper could hope for was that Filor was safe and travelling unhindered. Considering the enormity of her task, it brought Whisper sharply back to her own commitment within their partnership. She stood and whispered to herself, "Travel safe and may the kings of Balagh protect you." After a prolonged stare she turned and covered the short distance to the commencement of the climb. It was a steep climb to the narrow ledge. There was an open face to the right before a sharp turn to the left. From there, it rose to, where she hoped, it ended in an exit out of the gorge.

She scaled the first rock which sat at the very entrance to the path like a large marble lodged in a narrowed tube. Jumping up and over the initial obstacle, she commenced the climb. She did not rely on small bushes or protruding roots as her first line answer to her much-needed speed to intercept the Tronta troop. She recognised the bushes and knew from her experiences in Balagh that their roots were short and easily removed. Therefore, any weight applied would be fraught with risk and a fall from this height would certainly be fatal.

She pushed herself against the wall as she ascended. Sand and rock gave way under her long paws. The loosened pieces tumbled down the steep bank and out of sight. The distant sound of impact indicated the peril of the climb. She covered the distance by continually edging along the ledge. Her primary fear was the real possibility of stopping and being unable to start again. A paralysing fear lurked in her head and probed for a weakness with malice intent. She was fuelled to press on, not by her own mortality, but one of not completing her side of her agreement with Filor. And bigger than that, the death of all those who remained in Balagh. At this point they were blissfully unaware of the menacing threat that was coming from the east.

After a short and dangerous turn to the right, the narrow ledge widened up to the summit. Upon reaching the top, her breaths were heavy. She turned and scanned the land to the south. At this height she could see in all directions. The spine of rocks was the standout feature as if vertebrae running through the centre of a sunburnt back; rigid, firm and strong. The river closely followed the rocky nodules as if a vein carrying its blood. She took a deep breath in from the hard climb and her nostril's sensitive cells picked up various smells from the openness that now surrounded her. The difference couldn't have been starker from the valley below where the foliage was claustrophobic.

The scents on the high platform where crisp, fresh and light having been carried from the open vastness around her. She could almost smell the sweetness in various colours of reds, yellows and greens that surrounded her, from the small flowers to the green in the high leaves in the sporadic trees' canopies.

Whisper's mood lifted and her thoughts turned to Filor and how far she and the Clais troop had travelled south. Her thoughts then turned to her task and how far north Tronta and Thulo had travelled along the distant jagged spinal range. Her primary mission had not changed. It was to stop Tronta and have them return to the south to defend their home. All of a sudden the deafening silence was broken by two rapid cracking sounds that reverberated around the rocks before falling silent again. She scanned the distant skies searching for any familiar lightning or storm activity, but there was none. The skies were dark with rain clouds amassed in the distance. In the vastness she was quickly drawn to glints of light in a small opening next to the river.

She focused on the two objects, which although small, moved with purpose and fast. Her mouth dropped open as she realised it was those who were to be feared above all others. "Tall Walkers," she whispered, unsure how good their hearing was. She recounted stories of weapons that could kill without sight. How they travelled in large noisy beasts where they were consumed as if swallowed and spoke in a strange tongue. As she studied them she realised they were also heading south and appeared to be following the river. A cold shiver ran down her spine. Her neck fur stood erect. The thought of how the Tall Walkers could be following Filor made her stomach lurch. What could she do? Descend the hill again? To follow the river south in the hope of finding her friend again?

In her fevered contemplation on what to do, Whisper realised Filor now faced a double threat to her life; one from the tall walkers and the other from the Clais troop. Whisper hopped forward, determined to save her friend whose life was now in imminent danger. On approaching the ledge back down to the stream, she stopped with a jolt as an alternative thought and vision appeared. The destruction of family and friends lying blood-soaked and lifeless across Balagh's golden sand, now tarnished red. She visioned Clais standing in the cave on the platform which belonged to father and his forefathers.

She visioned her father slumped, humiliated, beaten, bleeding and the Clais troop surrounding him with laughter while they mocked and kicked.

She stood rocking backward and forward on her thick tail for a moment before she turned to face the large ridge of red spinal rock that was now only a short distance away. She loved Filor but the threat to her home, family and friends may end Balagh and the freedom of these lands. It could not fall into the hands of Clais and all the evil it would entail. The only chance of survival for Balagh and Filor was to have the Tronta troop return. With this new determination, she headed back up the gentle slope and refocused, hopping quickly between the bushes. As she approached the bottom of the next climb, the red rock shimmered in the glow of the sun's rays between the clouds which illuminated her way. On the other side of the climb she hoped to find Thulo, Tronta, Gribe and the battle-ready troop. With this thought, her excitement built. The tiredness was replaced with urgency and a newfound energy. She placed her first paw north which was then followed by the next and she became quicker and quicker as she ascended the bank with powerful determined bounds. With a clear line of sight, she leant forward and said, "Thulo, here I come."

The top of the climb came into view as Whisper's lungs and legs worked in unison. Any tiredness was ignored as she approached the top breathing heavily. On summiting the embankment, she turned and leaned on a rock to catch her breath as she peered through squinted eyes. The sun shone unhindered by any cloud and was a bright orbed orange as it headed down towards the distant skyline. Like an eye surrounded by a blue iris, she felt it was staring back at her, lighting the way before the moon and darkness fell. As if understanding, she turned and moved off quickly. The final warm breeze of the day pushed and guided her as if it was a gentle friendly hand of hope on her back.

Northward Bound

Thulo lay on the warm soil. The troop were scattered in the shadows of the overhang and had rehydrated. He lay facing the opening which now stood large and imposing in the distance. Thulo had never seen it before and was in awe at how high the large rocky ridge stood before almost ending in a vertical abruptness. After a short gap it rose again steeply before continuing its southerly travels back to Balagh. Shining like a beacon, there stood a high arch of rock that spanned the gap, connecting the two and framing the world beyond. He had not known this arch existed. The reality of their protective unity in its defence of Balagh, reassured him. To see the two great undulating walls joined like this provided him with some deep incomprehensible comfort as if the walls were joined in the form a strong paw shake of trusted friendship.

The troop talked with an air of anticipation about meeting their comrades from the east and south. Over the years, they had become the most trusted of friends and were known to be fierce uncompromising warriors and would surely prove the difference in battle. Thulo noticed there was little talk of the loss of Elimir, to the Tall Walker trap. Upon reflection, he decided this was because they would see him again when their time came. Little was also spoken about the impending battle from an individual standpoint. There was a resigned acceptance there would be death, pain and sadness. But he had no doubt they all believed mortality was a small sacrifice to pay for the greater good of Balagh. The hum of individual words reached his ears as he lay silent and alone. Each separate word had meaning, depending on the depth of tone and urgency of those speaking. He heard words like death, bite, anger, hunger, love, weather and tired. Although they meant nothing to Thulo in singular context, they were all interwoven into the fabric of conversations taking place across the troop. The words ebbed away into a muffle as his thoughts effortlessly drifted to holding Filor in a warm unbreakable embrace by the mirrored billabong.

Alone, he sat and leant against a large, concave rock. He felt so far from home, so far from what was his normal life and routine. There was a pleasant warmth within him, a recognition of how lucky he had been. A loving mother, who in the time he had with her, had learnt about accepting who he was, appreciation for all that surrounded him, to dream big and to care.

His mind drifted to his father who was equally loving, strong, committed and a planner. Yes, almost a visionary but with unwavering passion and devotion.

Then there was Whisper. He instinctively smiled as her large eyes appeared in his mind, excited, full of boundless opportunity and wonderment. He wished he had her here now. She would make things all right, take away his worries as for her, there were never any challenges, just opportunities waiting to be gathered in both paws and explored.

There was Gribe, yes Gribe, his inner voice repeated. He wondered where it had all gone so wrong with him. What had he done to upset Gribe so much? They used to get on so well, laugh even. Frustration and annoyance now pulsated through him. The warmth in his stomach from his previous thoughts was now replaced with burning acid. He quickly stood, alert once again.

Now it was dark, the large rock upon which he leant cast even darker shadows around it. He moved off, his mind awash with possible reasons for the breakdown in their relationship. Weaving his way between the rocks and scrub, he approached a large and very tired looking tree. Its canopy was dry and brittle, its bark withered from the unrelenting heat. Unbeknown to Thulo, at the very thickest part of the tree's trunk sat a large, rusted chain. Silent, it sat cold and coiled like a snake hidden in thick scrub which lay at the exit point out of the enclave.

With slow hops, Thulo paid little attention as the thoughts continued to swirl. Pawing the ground with his strong claws, he passed the tree. He leant forward, placed his front paws on the hard stoney ground between the sharp needles in the thick scrub and took his weight through his shoulders to pass through.

"Stop," said a voice from behind the tree. It was said with such urgency it made him instantly freeze. From behind the tree appeared Gribe, his face serious and concentrated. He did not look at Thulo but felt around the base of the tree with care.

"What are you doing?" Thulo asked, annoyed.

Gribe did not answer. Suddenly he stopped and looked up at Thulo. With a clanging sound of frustrated metal, Gribe straightened and in his hand swung the same rusted red teethed monster, the large contraption open and ready to close upon any passing limb. He dropped it to the ground where it snapped shut with a powerful clang.

Thulo stood open-mouthed and stared at Gribe who stood with unblinking eyes.

"Come," Gribe said, "we have much to discuss." And with a look he had once given in their younger fun-loving days, he moved off and after a momentary pause Thulo duly followed.

The Cloaked Protector

"Father entrusted me to look after you, be your guide and protector. He didn't need to ask me, Thulo, I would have protected you anyway." Gribe fell silent again.

Thulo did not speak as he absorbed the words and the love he was being shown.

"I have always looked out for you and have always known you to be the future King when father relinquishes his crown," Gribe added.

Thulo faced his brother. They stared at each other and for the first time Thulo could see his brother for who he really was. The hardness and assumed dislike were gone. His body was free and relaxed, his eyes warm and shining, alive.

"I thought you didn't like me," said Thulo. "You've always been," there was a pause, "you've always been a little … hard."

Gribe smiled warmly.

Thulo stared at him, the frown for which he had become accustomed had been replaced with a softness to his features. "I just wanted to protect you, keep you safe and wrongly or rightly, I thought by pretending to be the next in line I would be the target of any retaliation."

"But you could have been hurt or even killed," said Thulo, realising the enormity of the cloaked act.

Gribe took a small hop forward and looked stern. "Thulo, as your brother I will always stand by your side, lay down my life for you." He paused. "That's why father has entrusted your care and guidance to both Tronta and myself."

Thulo tried to place the last two and half years into some kind of sequential order that made any sense. As thoughts flickered, it dawned on him how this plan had been so well implemented from his birth to where he now stood. His thoughts ran through the years in a sequence of life events.

In doing so, he recognised how each of his family and friends had played their part in guiding him whilst protecting him from harm.

Gribe hopped forward, placed his paws on Thulo's shoulders and gripped him firmly. "This battle is but a chapter in your life's journey of experiences. Experiences you will learn from and build upon as King." He chuckled a deep fruity laugh as he finished the sentence. "You will protect our home, our legacy and further build relationships with our friends and comrades outside of these high walls, once this is all over. As with all kings who have led before, you will be an inspiration for our young to follow, prosper and be a beacon of light to show how all should live and love together. And on that journey, I will be with you every hop of the way."

Thulo pulled him in close and they hugged. It was filled with love that only brothers could share. As they separated, they both burst into laughter with a warmth and mateship that was almost overwhelming.

When a solitary cloud drifted across the moon's face they both looked up. The cloud was fully illuminated as if a torch were being shone through a bright white sheet. As Thulo and Gribe continued to talk and laugh, they fell silent when seventy hops to their right, small stones tumbled from somewhere up high. Gribe called in a whisper to three of his trusted warriors who joined them. They all peered up, trying to make sense of where the noise had originated from. Having seen them fall silent, further boomers joined the small group and stared skywards.

Their stares were accompanied by self-made misty clouds rising from their snouts. Each warrior billowed a warm misty plume as they snorted, each momentarily held before dissipating into the cold night sky. A gentle breeze pushed the cloud to continue its lonely journey south. As the moon peeped out, the land slowly lightened up as eager beams shone down. The light edged along the rock face as the cloud moved and was almost at the perceived point of where the stones had fallen and they stared in silent anticipation.

The moon's beam seemed to intensify as they braced themselves for what it may reveal. Approaching them, high on the ridgeline, the light revealed a solitary shape of a kangaroo. Each one of them gasped as there, looking down at them with the broadest of smiles, was their sister and friend to many, Whisper.

The News

With a cheeky laugh, Whisper shouted down. "At last, what took you so long?'

Still speechless, they continued to stare. The rest of the troop now joined them with interest and those who saw her were equally astonished. Suddenly and without warning Whisper disappeared. As the remaining troop continued to arrive with concerned interest, their confusion was doubled. Looking around at their comrades, they tried to make sense of the startled faces which mouthed voiceless words, whilst pointing at a ridgeline which appeared remarkably unexciting. They broke into low discussion as to whether the heat was now playing games with their imaginations.

"Boo!"

They all jumped with a start and turned to see Whisper behind them.

Some of the troop instinctively took a hop to the side, some clutched their chests and a few briefly clinched in a comforting hug, before releasing each other with a firm slap on the back and deep voices. From deep within the now packed group, there was a clear *squeak*, however the owner remained silent with multiple deep snorts coming from its rough location as if clearing a throat. Hopping from the group, Tronta, Gribe and Thulo moved slowly forward as if still in disbelief. Tronta stopped just short of where Whisper stood bouncing with excitement whilst Thulo moved forward and hugged her tight.

Whisper hugged him back. Being twins, their embrace communicated all that needed to be said at how they were both well and safe. Before they could separate, Gribe threw his arms around them both and squeezed tight. As they separated, they were all conscious of the many eyes that now stared at them.

Whisper looked at Gribe who was grinning broadly and turned to face Thulo who mouthed, "I will tell you later."

"What are you doing here, how did you get here?" asked Tronta with little emotion but full of urgent concern.

Whisper straightened her back, her previous thoughts of hunger, thirst and blistered paws diminished. So, this is how it felt to be listened to: truly listened to. Not just polite interest and a departing laugh. This is how it felt to stand equal, to be important and worthy of silence and concentration of all who stood staring in front of her. She purposely delayed speaking to prolong the feeling; one she knew she very much liked. However, this was not the night for self-importance.

"I have been travelling for one sun and this moon," she said, "I have not been alone, I was with Filor."

Thulo suddenly felt weak as every muscle and ligament went limp and his body sagged at the very mention of her name. The words *I was with* was all he heard, repeating over and over in a loud rhythmical beat. Those three simple words implied she was not at her side, not upon the ridge waiting to come down. At best she was injured and alone out there in the darkness or unconceivably dead.

Whisper continued to talk. Her words began to penetrate the thick soup that sloshed inside his head. He heard her name again.

"We had to separate and she has headed south to warn Broadback."

He heard Tronta speak with urgency. "Clais is heading south, are you sure, how can you be certain?"

Whisper detailed what they had witnessed. "We watched him along the river. He has a large troop of greys and reds. I assume he will cross and attack from the east when Balagh is weak and Broadback is alone."

Tronta looked stern and after a momentary pause he moved away in silence into the dark shadows of the rocks.

When his thoughts cleared Thulo said, "Filor's alive, she's okay, she's travelling alone, following Clais?" Thulo was aware of the speed in which he asked the questions but evidently his mouth had grown a brain of its own.

"Yes, she's fine," said Whisper. "Since your departure all she has wanted is to be with you, be part of the battle, stand by your side."

Thulo searched the darkness for Tronta who had been consumed by the shadows and was no longer visible. The troop were discussing their options which were split. Continue north to meet their allies the Kings and return in strength or return south to defend their home, outnumbered, but likely to meet the threat.

Flight and Fight

The animated discussion fell to a silence as Tronta, his arm swinging in line with his purposeful hop, appeared out of the darkness. As he approached, the light from the moon lit his face and his accompanying persona was dark and menacing. In stony silence he stood in front of the troop, looking at each of his boomers in turn. His eyes were ablaze in contrast to the night sky which was deep and dark.

"We return to Balagh tonight as we have no time to lose. We have to prepare ourselves that we may already be too late. Clais has a considerable start, our advantage however lies in that we travel direct. Clais is travelling south along the river before he crosses to enter Balagh. With the rain over our travel north the river will be swollen. He will have little option than travel far to the south where the river will narrow" He looked at them all with pride and purpose. "Take your fill of water for we leave immediately."

There was a sudden hum of noise across the troop who moved in excited huddles, a palpable excitement in the air. Gribe beckoned Thulo and Whisper to his side and they approached Tronta who stood under the tree, as he would have done in Balagh.

They stood in silence before Gribe spoke. "What about King Trigor and Grolt, we may need them in the battle?"

After a long silence Tronta spoke. "Whisper advises that the Clais troop is large." He looked grim as Whisper confirmed the statement with a nod. "Send Lombard, he is our quickest. The entrance is only half a night's travel. Assuming they have arrived early and they believe what is being said and leave immediately, they may just be what we need to win the fight or bury the dead." These last words were spoken with sadness as it dawned on them all the reality of the situation. Tronta instructed Gribe to mass the troop and ready them for the return home and prepare them for war on their arrival. Tronta summoned Lombard and upon his arrival, they moved to stand alone under a tree.

Thulo noticed the urgency in Tronta. He was highly animated, his good arm pointing and waving forcibly. Lombard hung on every word in nodding silence. Tronta finished his instruction, placed his paw on Lombard's shoulder and they both touched heads before Lombard moved off.

Thulo stood looking at Lombard, who on finishing his talk with Tronta, turned and headed in his direction. Thulo had seen Lombard many times whilst living in Balagh but had no memory of ever talking meaningfully with him.

Lombard stood in front of Thulo. "I am leaving now."

Thulo noted his voice was clear, concise and calm.

"I will meet our comrades to the north as planned and return to Balagh for battle." He firmed his stance and stood tall. "I shall not fail and I will fight side-by-side upon my return." Although shorter than Thulo, he was far leaner with powerful thighs clearly built for speed. His eyes were fierce with determination, and he did not leave any doubt that he had every intention of succeeding in the task bestowed upon him. He stared at Thulo, bowed his head, and paused before turning and re-joining a small group of his close comrades who had been watching with interest.

Before Lombard reached his friends they collectively turned and bowed their heads in Thulo's direction. After a brief discussion and forceful pat to his back from Tronta, Lombard moved off quickly with purpose and poise.

With the sun now peeking over the horizon they all watched as Lombard covered the ground quickly. Dust rose on every powerful impact. He skilfully navigated the land with ease, covering a large distance with each long bounding leap with elegance and poise. Thulo noted how low Lombard's upper body was. His short upper muscular arms held tight to his side and were ejected forward at every hop before recoiling back next to his body like tuned pistons. His lean, muscular hind legs and long paws shot forward before his large claws dug deep into the dry red dirt. Once dug deep and with his low gait, his hind legs propelled him forward before repeating the process again with fluidity and efficient effectiveness. His long muscular tail almost acted as a rudder that adjusted as Lombard skilfully changed direction to avoid any rock or bush that would slow his building speed.

They stood in awe as he was soon lost in the peaks of orange and the darkness that lay thick on the horizon.

Tronta called out to speak with the troop and they massed around him. They huddled in the last remaining shadows of the rocks as the darkness retreated under the new sun's glare.

"This call to arms is to protect Balagh, which is now under threat like never before. All we have worked so hard for, all we have built and grown together - they aim to destroy, decimate all you love and take everything as their own." His voice rose in depth and anger. "We are all that stands between Clais and the change that will veil our land in evil and despair forever. We may be outnumbered." He paused and hopped closer as the troop also hopped closer to him. "But we have unity, togetherness." He moved yet closer. "We are family. Clais' troop is fractured, broken, there will be division between the reds and the greys. We will work to divide them and once their unity is broken we will drive home our advantage, kill Clais and rid this world of the north raiders forever. Clais is self-absorbed. His arrogance cannot see what is clearly before him. His hatred has made him weak. His weakness is our strength."

On these strong words, the troop roused with pride and purpose. They snorted deep and loud, and scraped the dry earth with their claws, each clearly roused at the speech. Each looked fierce and intense, all seeming to have grown at least a foot. Tronta stood and stared with an aura of a battle-hardened warrior who was ready to kill without pity or remorse. He turned. The sun was now half visible. Without further words he hopped off a small ledge and the troop kept pace with his every lolloping leap as they headed south, to battle.

Prying Eyes

Filor and Hale moved up the bank in slow motion, remaining cautiously silent, unseen and undetected to eye and smell. Their fear was that Clais may have left one of his troop on the southerly path to ensure they were not being followed. Another concern was whether the Clais troop had even passed the point they were about to breach. Having been carried down the river in such a fast flow meant the distance travelled was unknown. Their confusion lay in that very question. Had Hale travelled so far down the river that they had caught or passed those they pursued.

The bank they climbed was steep and as such they grabbed at branches and dug their claws deep into the mud which oozed thick and wet between their paws. Thankfully, the heavy rain had made the branches pliable enough they bent wilfully under the weight of being grasped. Had the rain not fallen the same grasped branches would likely have snapped and surely alerted the troop to their presence. When they neared the top of the bank, they instinctively lowered their height and hid between weeping foliage. They allowed enough provision in their exposure to see through the gaps in the sagging leaves and with dark wet fur they were camouflaged well to their surroundings.

Hale glanced back at the river which had tried to take her life. It continued to bubble a few hops away. In the water's spit and froth, it spoke to Hale that should she return for a second time, there would be no escape. Hale was also acutely aware of what had happened to the large boomers who had been sent forward by Clais to kill her. The whistle she had clearly heard when it flew past her head, and the resulting impact was both vivid in her memory and smell. Although both towered above her and were full of hate, they were no match for the objects the tall walkers hit them with.

The threat to their lives in pursuit of Clais was now very real from both sides of the river. As they lay low whispering about their next move, the muffled roar of the river was replaced with the sounds of movement and the hum of voices to their front.

Lying even lower to the ground, Filor and Hale picked visual points between the foliage and peered out unblinking. Deep in the trees' shadows the Clais troop moved in silence. The colours of dark grey and red mottled through the canopy. The ad-hoc movement due to their varying heights, gave the impression of a large grotesque insect contorting, bloating and contracting as if one long cylinder. The troop continued slowly and disappeared around the next bend which took them further inland and away from the river.

Filor caught Hale's eye. "Now we have a reference point," she whispered, a communication they had both agreed to under the circumstances.

"We have to move quickly. They are only one moon and sun away from Balagh," Filor added.

From their high vantage point looking back across the river, the distant forked V-shape of where their home sat could just be seen. "We will have to get to the other side as quickly as we can and try and make a direct line home." Hale pointed.

"But the river is so wide. How are we going to cross? It is too dangerous here. We would never make it," said Filor with a panicked urgency.

The river roared as if listening and begging them to try. They crept through the foliage with constant glances behind to ensure there was no sign of the tall walkers. Ensuring they were alone, they moved cautiously around the bank. The river rushed around a large arc to the left, effectively heading away from Balagh before a distant bend to the right could just be made out. The river was wide and wild. The only possible point that could be seen with a slight narrowing, lay in the distance where the river ran wide before rounding another bend. On approaching the narrowed section there stood several large grey gnarled stones which bridged its width to the far side bank.

Each protruding stone stood gapped and out of alignment. Each was chipped, gnarled and decaying where the river, over thousands of years, had eroded the gaps which created a look of decaying teeth. What was left of the stones, however, stood firm.

The water passing through the gaps was sluggish, although on the outside the river raged in anger at these annoying obstacles.

"There's our point of crossing" said Hale, trying to sound positive. "There's the weakness, but it's not without risk."

Filor remained silent as she scanned the crossing. "It's dangerous but we have no other option if we want to get back to Balagh."

They eyed each other.

"We can do this," said Hale.

Filor took a deep breath, "Balagh depends on it."

Sweat, Flies and Pen

"This is where we are," said George, placing a single fingertip on a brown golden point on the crinkled map. "And this is where we viewed the large gathering of roos on the riverbank and that seven-footer." His finger slid across the river into the small opening of green and brown which highlighted trees and gradient. "They appeared to be heading south which gives us a great opportunity ... right here."

His finger followed the river's flow to a high peaked point which overlooked the river. A narrow gully of flat land sat between the elevated platform and a steep high wall. "If we get there first we may have the upper hand with a clear line of sight." He scratched at the grey whiskers that bristled loudly, having sprouted from his unshaven chin.

Bob opened the buttoned pocket in his shirt and pulled out the trusted black marker. He circled the narrowing which encompassed the trees that sat opposite the high wall. On the other side sat the unmistakable large blue circle which indicated a billabong. "Right, to confirm, we travel down the right side of the river. Cross over here where the river narrows, either with the car or on foot, and head straight for this elevated ridge. He tapped his finger on the black penned ring which vibrated through the grey faded tray.

From there they agreed they would walk up the small incline and bed themselves in the congregation of trees which sat opposite the forked outcrop. "We should have a clear sight of the roos, assuming this is the direction they take to the billabong."

They folded up the old map and eagerly returned to their seats. Bob placed the map in the sun visor under the discoloured stretched strap which now hung loose. George wound the window up and turned up the A\C. The car coughed into life and Bob signalled the direction to take and they slowly moved off.

Broken Teeth, Hungry River

Now a plan had been set, Filor and Hale hopped along the bank with renewed vigour. Both knew the importance of crossing the river and gaining time on Clais, although fraught with risk. They were also aware of the danger that lurked below. The rippled peaks and troughs in the river created small white hungry points on their random, disorganised impact. These points gave the appearance of a gaping mouth filled with hundreds of teeth, each eagerly waiting to grip tight on their prey.

"Are you okay?" Hale asked.

Whisper was a little distance behind with her head bowed, clearly focused on securing her footing. "Yeah, I'm okay," she said quietly without looking up.

The river continued to roar below, inaudible words shouted, white froth spraying like spittle. Suddenly and out of nowhere, there came a roar, not a natural sound like thunder or falling rock and they both stopped in unison, breathing heavily. Hale slowly turned to face Whisper who met her wide-eyed stare. Her pupils dilated, ears retracted, the sound was like none they had ever heard before.

Appearing from the north, the clearly identifiable tall walkers moved in their large oddly shaped beast. It travelled without legs, noisy, awkward but strong. It had clearly crossed the river as it was wet and covered in mud.

Whisper's sensitive nose twitched as a strange smell wafted from the beast. They both instinctively stared without thought as the monster rounded a rock and both it and the sound of whatever it was, faded and disappeared out of sight.

Scared, Whisper slowly moved towards Hale. Leaning forward and slightly overstretched she grabbed a small shrub which bent under the grip and her weight. With a jump, a clump of mud folded under the pressure exerted in her hind legs.

Whisper's leg straightened with the collapse and with the steepness of the bank she slipped and fell. Sliding uncontrollably, she screamed, "Hale." The bank further down gave way under her sliding weight. The mud and sand carried her to the water which lapped and frothed hungrily.

Hale covered the distance in three leaps and with each, the soil under paw gave way with the force applied. Leaping, she slid down the bank, reached out and grabbed Whisper who fumbled for her paw before grabbing it tightly with panicked force. They looked at each other with eyes filled with fear.

Hale grabbed for anything to slow their tumble. Wet branches simply gave way at the root. Hale kicked again and with the propelled momentum, grabbed Whisper, who embraced her in a full hug. Together they hit a large rock which propelled them into the air before they splashed into the water. Water splayed into the air before swallowing them whole in a large brown muddy mouth. The cold impact stole their breaths. The abrupt shock and power of the water separated them from each other's embrace.

Hale opened her eyes with a squint. Black and brown water swirled through the tiny gap and filled her eyes with grit. She closed them tight and fought to reach the surface as her brain screamed for air. She kicked and without knowing her direction of travel, broke the surface and took a large rasping gasp. Cold air filled her lungs before the water plunged her under again. Spinning, she broke the surface, and in that brief second of reprieve, searched for any sign of Whisper. As she plunged under yet again, her brain slowed and focused on whether any of the momentary visions had Whisper in them. The water grabbed and pulled her as she fought to reach the riverbank.

The water's grasp and swell kept her in the centre of its flow where she was weak and vulnerable. Suddenly she hit a rock and all air left her once more. Water rushed into her mouth, filling every corner and searching out any pockets of air that might sustain her fight for life. Lights exploded in her head and with each flash and pop there was a reality and a realisation that death was imminent. Her struggle to gain air waned, her limbs slowed as a kind voice whispered. "Let go, relax, the pain will stop soon, warmth and love are not far away."

Suddenly there was a deep plunging sound and a frantic grab as she was propelled upwards through the water. She broke the surface at speed and hit her head hit on a cold rock. Opening her eyes, there stood a Whisper highlighted by the sun.

Whisper thrust her face forward, her green eyes wide, kind, caring but full of urgency. "Come on," she said and pulled hard. She lifted Hale out of the water onto a small rock platform.

Hale hung onto the rock with spayed paws and unable to speak. She coughed as waves of shivers ran down her body. "Than … th … thank you," she stammered between coughs. The river below bounced up the rock with feeble fingers hoping to pull them back in with clear frustration. Hale's breath slowed and with that her mind cleared. "Where are we?" The warm fingers of the sun prodded her coat in a vain attempt to return circulation to her extremities.

"We're on the rocks. The ones we looked at from the bank at the narrowing."

"Okay," said Whisper, "are you able to stand? We need to move and get ourselves out of sight as those Tall Walkers could be nearby."

These words ignited Hale with an inner strength that pulsed through her capillary network with a jolt.

Standing on the small ledge they both clung tight. "Look," said Whisper, pointing at grip points and a craggy ledge on the next protruding rock. With confidence she leapt and clung tight, moving to its rear to allow room for Hale.

With hesitancy and head still hurting and a taste of blood in her mouth, Hale leapt. She landed hard, bounced off the rock and leant backward with a jolt.

Whisper reached forward and pulled her back. "That's twice," she said with a smile.

Two large protruding rocks remained for them to clear before they could reach the bank and safety. The final two obstacles, although closer together, provided a portal for the water to rush through with a torrential ferocity. Whisper looked back at Hale. The sun reflected from her white fur and a confidence shone in her eyes. She smiled again with assuring warmth before leaping onto the rock.

Hale saw Whisper land on the second to last rock before automatically leaping to the next without hesitation and then onto the muddy bank and the safety of firmer ground.

All Hale could see and hear was the water spitting and calling her name in loud booming bursts. She closed her eyes and gripped tight. The voice of her father spoke and she sensed his presence, followed by an embrace that for the briefest of moments hugged her tight. Eyes still closed and lost in the memory; she was certain she could smell him.

"Don't be scared, you have work to do and Balagh's survival depends on you getting off these rocks, now move."

Hale opened her eyes, took a deep breath and leapt.

Bounding Home

Lombard covered the land quickly, each jump measured, featherlike but packed with power. His focus was on returning to Balagh to save not only his King but family and friends with whom he had grown up. The thought of failure was overpowered, engulfed by one of success. Each jolt through his legs generated a vivid picture of his friends, family, the billabong, Broadback and his promise to Thulo and Tronta. The arch was no longer a distant squint, but full and open and loomed large.

Lombard had never been this far from Balagh. The rock walls were wide and the ground upon which he bounded, levelled off. The rocks under paw dissipated and the warmth in the soft sand was a welcome relief to his padded paws. He became conscious of a drop in temperature in the shadows of the rocks which towered all around him. The land which moments before had been bright, now fell to dark orange and deep shadowed reds. He also became very aware of the echoes from his bounding hops, all thoughts of stealth unavoidably lost. He wondered if the reverberating sounds around the high rock faces were in fact them talking with each other upon his arrival. As he slowed, he suspected his presence would have been a little out of the ordinary in this distant lonely land where the thoroughfare of life would have been minimal. As he approached the entrance, his heart thrummed in anticipation of meeting the hardened and war hungry warriors and Kings before heading south to save Balagh. He passed under the high arch of rock which framed the open land beyond and wet his lips to speak when greeted by the Kings and comrades. He momentarily gazed at the distant landscape which was tinged with green after the recent rains. As he passed through he slowed when the heat in his paws grew as the sun breached the shadowed defences on this side of the high steep wall. Silence pounded in his ears. He looked left and right as a cool breeze passed low in a welcoming gust. His fur swayed in the wind which soon penetrated through to his skin which was welcome before settling flat once again as it raced on.

He stood alone. The excitement drained from him as his wish to be met by pats and questions slowly dissipated. In this moment of solitude, his mind quickly joined his friends and family who were heading into a massacre. He suddenly felt sick and without warning he vomited and continued retching long after all of the contents were expelled. Standing, he wondered if he would be able to head back with the required urgency as the energy he'd felt upon arrival, had now completely drained from him.

His mind whirled on what to do as his choices were limited and stark. Head back to Balagh and be with those he loved or stay and wait for the troops to arrive. The scenario of the troops not being present and ready to immediately leave in defence of Balagh had not been discussed with Tronta.

"What should I do?" he asked out loud, licking his nose and moistening his lips once again with minimal effect. He dropped his head and closed his eyes. Another gust of wind ran through and although he was standing in the sun, he suddenly felt cold. He turned and looked back towards home where he could just about make out the rock landmarks which would lead him there. He stood tall and opened his eyes with a decision made. He moved off, passing under the archway for the final time, picking up speed as he headed for home. No matter the outcome, he wanted to be with his kin to fight and fall or rejoice. But either way they would be together.

He moved quickly, now fully committed to his new mission, letting Tronta and Broadback know they would fight alone. As he moved from the dark shadows into the sun he became aware of the unnatural shadowing that lay on the sand all around him. As he bounded, he realised the shapes did not belong to high defined edges that he had known for the entirety of his life. The high uneven shadows were out of place. He had learnt to develop this skill of observing for outplaced objects or lines whilst playing ghosting in his younger days and later in combat practice with Tronta. He slowed to a stop and turned, searching the low open sparseness behind and the arch which was now some 100 hops away and bathed in half light. He stood squinting until his eyes adjusted to the differing light. Suddenly to his left, a stone tumbled and ricocheted as it bounced off the rock and sent echoes pinging across the walls to his left and right. Looking up with his mouth open, he sagged at his knees and took three hops' forwards.

On the high walls stood at least sixty strong warriors. They looked fearsome, strong, determined and silent.

The large boomer to the right asked, "Who are you?" his voice deep and echoing for all to hear.

"I am Lombard, a close friend of Tronta."

There was a sudden murmuring amongst those who looked down upon him. The king raised his paw and they fell silent.

"Where is Tronta? We expected him to be here to stand beside us in the battle" the other asked.

Lombard looked down and gathered his thoughts before looking up purposefully. "He is leading the troop south to Balagh." His eyes swept left and right to show equal respect to the Kings. "We have received news that Clais has headed south along the river to Balagh and plans to attack from the west."

There was another murmur, this time more animated. The two Kings eyed each other with concern clearly etched on their faces. "Where did you hear this news?

"Whisper," answered Lombard. "She travelled with Filor to join the battle at the opening. On their journey north on the far side of the wall they came across Clais and his Troop of Greys and Reds heading south. They number around seventy."

There was a momentary silence.

"Where is Filor now?"

"She has headed south to stand by her father in battle. Tronta instructed me to come to the opening and deliver his message."

"When was Clais last seen?"

"Two suns ago," Lombard replied, with a resigned tone.

Silence fell before the King to the right spoke. "If he is heading South, following the river, he will need to cross at a narrowing far down its flow. He will then head westerly before sweeping easterly where high cliffs of Balagh join the river." He paused again. "He has opted for surprise with a longer route travelled. If we leave now and without pause we may still have time to defend Balagh."

The two kings eyed each other, while the troops who surrounded them remained silent awaiting their King's command.

"Broadback and Tronta are our closest friends. Warrior Lombard we are coming down."

The troop turned and moved out of sight. Lombard gulped, trying to take in what was happening and what impact this might have in saving Balagh.

The troop appeared moments later, hopping in unison, well-drilled, well-trained, a formidable fighting force.

A strange warmth ran through Lombard as they approached, their size, demeanour and organisation were impressive. "Maybe, just maybe," he said quietly with excitement building.

The troop stopped in front of him. The resulting dust cloud continued its momentum as it carried on over him before dissipating in a gentle swirl.

"I am King Trigor, this is King Grolt."

They both moved forward, each in turn gripping his shoulders firmly before smiling. The kings both turned in unison to face their troops. "Our friend, Broadback, and Balagh are at even greater risk of death and destruction now that Clais attacks from the East. We will answer his call. We move with speed as we have little time to waste." They turned to face Lombard. "We will follow you."

Lombard turned and with the heaviness in his legs well and truly gone, he bounded off and under his breath said, "Broadback hold on, we are on our way. "

River Crossed

Clais stood opposite the narrowing in the river. The water at the narrow sandbank lapped gently, having passed over some large rocks which broke its momentum. The water between the banks arced in a large sweep that ran off to the right. Small, pebbled stones shimmered below the water; the flow notably slower on the outside as it carved its path. From the higher bank upon which he stood, the crossing seemed to be shallow on the distant bank. The high rock face that protected Balagh, cast a sweeping shadow into the open plain some 800 hops from the river.

As he approached the river's edge, shapes of differing sizes darted under the shallow water. Studying the bank opposite, a small cluster of trees stood at the base of a graduated climb that led directly into Balagh. Clais was conscious that the V-shaped narrowing would only allow one of his troop to pass through at a time. This would take some planning to ensure that what remained of the Broadback troop were not alerted to their presence as they massed on top. Two boomers moved to his side and followed his gaze across the river. His scarred lip quivered, spittle sitting thick at the corner of his mouth, small bubbles building and popping with each deep breath. He eyed them both in turn.

"Take the troop cross the river and have them quietly shelter within the trees. Sources have confirmed Broadback has already sent his troops north. He will not be prepared for our overwhelming assault. We will fortify Balagh for when Tronta returns, weary and ready to negotiate when he realises Broadback is defeated and we hold all the Broadback clan hostage with the promise of death unless our demands are met. We move at the rise of the new sun. Have the troop gather in the shade and rest in preparation for war. Once the assault begins, have the first twenty attack, then have the remainder follow in unison as we overwhelm them with our numbers. Broadback, his family, the young and elderly are to be spared for our negotiations with Tronta.

"What of Broadback?" one of the boomers asked with a husk.

Clais remained unmoved and continued his stare. "Broadback will lose his remaining eye to spend a life in darkness, and his family will be mine. His daughter, Whisper, will be my queen and together our offspring will be the next generation to rule Balagh under my rule of law."

His voice darkened. "Broadback will be banished and forgotten, broken, weak, meaningless." His eyes narrowed and his jaw muscles pulsed. His teeth protested at being ground together with considerable force. A thick mucus ran from his mouth into his neck fur.

Smale, one of the two commanders who stood next to Clais, broke the silence. "We have selected the first to assault Balagh." Smale was an older boomer, his fur a thick red and coarse, teeth gapped at the front with a quiet husky voice. However, each word selected was assured and confident with an air of experience and consideration. There were no wasted words, each chosen carefully for impact as if knowing with his aging years that he had few left to speak. "They are aware of your requirements. They will divide those who remain and cause maximum panic in those who try to defend." He paused.

"Go on," said Clais.

Smale continued with relish enjoying his moment in the spotlight. "They will be brutal, merciless. Broadback and his family will be spared but will be forced to witness the death and destruction before you arrive." Although the oldest of the troop, his lust for pain, brutality and death had not eroded. As he spoke, his words became excited in their rasping pitch and sadistic tone as his mind played out the horrors to come.

Clais's breathing also quickened as if he too was seeing the devastation, death and revenge that he had so long wished for in the story being told.

He fell silent in his own unblinking thoughts as he relived the trauma and overwhelming sadness he had felt in scooping his father's warm limp body from the ground where Broadback had left it, slumped and discarded. The resulting years he had spent without his father to watch over him and teach him the ways of ruling with authority stolen. The pain he had felt in his face as the wounds inflicted by Tronta never truly healed. Since the death of his father his wounds had wept pus, invited sucking flies, bled with a continual pain in every word spoken and every mouthful of food eaten. He had endured the continual dribble that matted his fur and exuded a pungent smell that never truly dried. How he had never met a true partner which he was sure was due to his disfigurement and those who had promised love looked at him with disguised disgust in their eyes. Knowing those he had been with only did so because of his name and the chance to elevate their status. He felt physically sick at how Broadback had continued to prosper, grow his family and broaden his lands through sickening friendships that meant nothing. When what was clearly needed was a firm hand of law and uncompromising strength of leadership and powerful retribution. He then recalled the texture and pungent smell of his father's blood which saturated his fur as they travelled the long road north.

He blinked quickly, dragging himself back from the deep-seated thoughts of pure hate. As he stared at the cold water, he retched a hot fluid which burnt the back of his throat at what Broadback had stolen from him. However, he had been patient in planning his retribution. He had visualised the attack, predicted Broadback and Tronta's likely defensive strategies which resulted in his counter strategic attack from the east. His father's passing was like a constant gnawing pain. An emptiness that ate at him like a chronic sickness that could only be ended by inflicting brutal, unbridled revenge. He barely slept. He was blind to the natural wonders that surrounded him. Living, to him, had become a chore. Darkness filled his every living breath and the sun never felt warm to him.

The troop crossed the shallow river. Each welcomed the gently rippling water that worked eagerly to clean the sand and stone from between their cracked pads. Reaching the far side, they climbed the short steep sandy bank and trailed each other in a line of silence. The greys and reds remained steadfast but in two tightly knit groups. The relationship between the two remained one of distrust and dislike. Each, throughout their journey south, had vied for position they deemed to be the most advantageous if the others were to suddenly attack.

On this occasion, the large lean reds took the lead across the river. They collectively planned this move, knowing the pressure on the shorter greys would be considerable, especially on exiting an increasingly muddy bank. The reds continually looked back at the greys as they crossed. Many hoped one or two might fall and be washed away to their deaths and didn't want to miss such a spectacle. The reds, already some distance ahead, having cleared the bank easily, laughed and whispered with each other which did not go unnoticed. Having reached the base of the sporadic trees quickly they sought and secured the limited shade cast by the trees' long branches and leafed canopy. They clumped together, emphasising how cool it was in the shade as the greys arrived to stand in the sun, panting, muddy and looking agitated as they swatted the eager flies away.

Broadback's Reflection

Broadback stood looking out across from his elevated platform within his cave. His mind was full of swirling emotion as he stared northwards. His thoughts were occupied by a scenario where Clais had reconsidered his planned attack and decided to remain and live the remainder of his life in happiness and maybe with a family of his own. In this scenario his troop and family returned home uninjured. To live their lives happy and free, without the burden of war hanging over them.

However, he also knew this hope was purely that. He had seen for himself the hate in Clais' eyes and knew that behind their darkness was deep hatred and the want for revenge. So, in the moments where the negative spin did slow and with a concerted effort, he envisaged a scenario of greeting them one by one from a victorious battle. In his perfect wish they had no injuries, there had been no deaths and Clais had once again been banished north or better still, killed. However, Broadback knew that in reality and supported by history, that in battle there would be death and the Balagh family would mourn every one of the brave fallen. His blue eye held within its reflection the setting sun which sat suspended. The sun's final rays stretched out to thin points as silvery shadows crept slowly forward and saturated the deep recesses of his thoughts. Looking to his left the still water at the far end of the billabong reflected perfectly the silver boab. The surrounding backdrop of the nights sky and glinting stars only added to its beautiful glory.

Broadback returned his gaze to the horizon, his mind once again swirling. His thoughts drifted to Whisper. His fiery, stubborn, fun loving and beautiful daughter. A born spirit with a desire for equality and to be respected and fiercely independent.

He had watched as Whisper and Filor quickly descended the steep slope and safe confines of Balagh, before disappearing into the night just a moon and sun ago. He stood unseen in the natural crevice of the narrow path hidden by its depth and resulting shade. His interest sparked by their increased meetings and intenseness of conversation since the departure of the main troop. He had his suspicions confirmed as he wandered over to a sandy spot where they had been in deep conversation before heading up the steep hill and disappearing out of view on being disturbed by a lurking Gribe. On the ground in the fine sand Whisper had used a claw to draw a diagram of the fork, a squiggly line which showed the wall, a further squiggle being the river and a large cross at the opening. He looked at the map in all of its innocence and naive inaccuracies. He could tell from its varying depths in its ingrains the excitement with which it had been drawn.

Broadback began to watch them more closely, although cautious not to make his increased keenness of observation noticeable. He noted that they both were making more time to take in their surroundings. It was if preparing they were preparing themselves that this maybe their last time Balagh. They were having lengthier talks with family and friends whilst spending longer periods of time reflecting on past stories with joy and laughter. The final indicator that something was planned was in a hug that Whisper had given him. On the evening prior to their departure and after their evening meal her parting embrace was noticeably different. He felt her grip to be firmer, burying her head deeper into his chest with a noticeable quickened breath as if holding back tears of sadness.

On pulling away she looked at him with a stare as if speaking words which were not spoken. As if unshackled from her plans and sworn silence she said, "I love you so much, father, you mean the world to me. I have learnt so much from you and no matter what happens I know you love me and I couldn't have asked for a better father or king." She went on staring intently into his eyes, "Thank you for the life and love you have given me and I will always, always love you."

"Are you okay Whisper, is there anything wrong,?' Broadback had asked.

"No, I'm fine, I just don't think I tell you enough that's all," and with a parting smile she turned and hopped off to join Filor who was gazing across the billabong. After a brief hug and animated discussion, they turned and headed out of sight into the darkening skies. Some hours later they descended the steep bank and vanished quietly into the night. He fought with every ounce of his parenting fibre not to stop them, in the full knowledge that they intended to travel north and fight with their brothers. He grimaced at the thoughts of what they would see: death, pain and blood which would likely change them forever, assuming they were not killed.

If he had intervened in stopping he would have effectively shackled the spirit that pulsed through her very being. By restricting her ambition and beliefs it would have only led to resentment, anger and frustration and a breakdown in their relationship. After many hours of deliberation, he concluded that he would rather her life be lived to its fullest, with happiness and love, than a life restrained by shackles and filled with sadness and frustration. This decision may ultimately mean that she may be injured or killed but in either scenario a life that would be celebrated as being full and honest. As she disappeared he hopped forward and placed his paw on the large warm rock. "Travel safe and may our forefathers protect you my child," before he bowed his head and swallowed hard.

Low Bank, Steep Climb

Standing together, they looked across to the distant outcrop of rocks. Filor's point of exit just a few suns and moons ago was now very visible once again. They both stood in silence with eyes on their home as warm memories flooded them equally. Filor reached for Hale's paw and they held each other with an unspoken understanding in the tightness of their grip.

They stooped low instinctively behind a narrow rock, short snouts leading to wide eyes. In the gentle breeze that blew in from the east, air particles carried scents from distant lands they could not yet see.

"That's Clais," said Hale. "I smelt him when he held me. I cannot mistake that foul pungent smell."

After a momentary pause, Filor said. "If that's Clais, his troops will be nearby."

Each resulting gust indicated they were close as the odour in the air grew ever more pungent. Travelling quietly along the riverbank they stopped.

"Shhh" said Filor as they both heard the quiet hum of hushed voices far off to their right.

"What do we do now?" asked Hale as they both peeked over the thick bushy riverbank. The troops were massed not far from the path they needed to climb to get back into Balagh. They returned to sit low and stare across the river having fallen into silence.

"So, as I see it there are two options," said Hale breaking the silence. "We continue to move along the riverbank where the river is at its loudest." They peered along the river's edge which was shallow with a small sand bank before rounding a sharp bend. "We will pass the Clais troop and continue to where the river meets the rock wall to Balagh." She pointed to reaffirm her plan. The red wall loomed large over them, although some 100 hops away in a straight line. "We will then move along the base in the darkness of the cave." Crouching low and peering through some low bush they could see it ran almost the entire length to the base of the climb. "We will wait for the right moment, climb as quick as we can, find Broadback and give him the news." On finishing Hale looked at Filo. "Do you have any other ideas?"

They discussed climbing the bank and going sharply to the right along the base of the rocky outcrop that sat directly opposite the Balagh entrance. But they concluded they would be in the open for way too long and likely be seen or smelt on any change in the wind's direction. In further discussion they also concluded the wind direction also supported the river plan strategy as the bank hid them well. As the planning discussion continued, they further surmised how their tracks would be harder to follow in the water if they were to be detected.

After the discussion they sat for a while and reaffirming the plan they held each other's paws firmly as they slowed their breaths and visualised what they had to do.

"Ready?" said Filor.

Hale nodded. They stood remaining stooped. Filor moved quickly to the water's edge, followed by Hale. They reached the sand and hopped into the water with caution. The dark water bubbled as it passed over some small rocks. Hale joined her and they moved along the water's edge where the slight decline in the bank worked to their advantage creating a further heightening within the bank. The mud under the shallow water squished and its thick deep consistency slowed their progress. The water was frigid cold and pushed on their thin hind legs. Every hop was purposeful to avoid any unnecessary noise that may indicate to listening ears, an unnatural presence which would warrant further investigation.

As they continued to move south, the cliff only grew to tower over them and the noise of muffled talking became unwelcomely louder. They quietly approached the point in which the troop had crossed the river. The mud was imprinted with deep padded prints which indicated significant weight and volume of numbers. They stopped, stooped and took small hops up the bank and peered over the top through a dense spiny bush. In the distance sat a clump of trees and amongst them were the scattered troop of Clais. Some of the boomers were lying, others stood alone, but most were in small groups no bigger than six and no smaller than three.

"Okay," said Hale in a whisper, with eyes on the river which was lit by the low-lying silver moon now a quarter of the way into the twinkling night sky.

A conversation louder than the distant hum, for which they had become attuned, approached and was heading towards the river's edge. Hale and Filor dropped to their chests and quickly pushed themselves into the overhang that had been carved out through years of high winter swells. As quick as a flash they dug sand out, flicking it into the river before pulling their legs in and falling silent. The thud of heavy paws could be heard and felt overhead. Each heavy placement vibrated through the small roots of shrubs that hung under the bank and swayed in front of them.

"I hate the greys," said a deep voice.

"They smell funny," came an equally deep voice and both laughed with a rasp. 'If I get a chance tomorrow, I'm going to kill a couple, break their scrawny necks with a simple snap. They will not be missed."

"Wasters, what are they even doing here anyway? We can win this fight on our own, we don't need their type living with us, pretending everything's okay. I say let's kill the Balagh troop then kill the greys and take Balagh for our own, we don't need to share with their kind."

"All the more for us," said the other.

Filo and Hale stared at each other, their eyes wide and unblinking.

"That's Clais' plan," said a hushed voice, "he has no loyalty to the greys. That's why he has brought them."

"He is only using them for their numbers to ensure we win the fight and then he will slaughter them all." They laughed with a horrible rumbling rasp. "They have no idea what's coming, this is our time and tomorrow we take Balagh for ourselves."

"I can't wait to see Broadback plead for mercy, snivelling, weak and broken."

"I can't wait to see Thulo slayed, the next king in waiting gone, the family line broken. And to finish it off we have Whisper to become Clais' wife." They both rattled another laugh before turning and moving off to re-join the group.

Filor sat frozen, hugging her hind legs as Hale straightened hers with a small sigh in relief. Hale reached out and grabbed Filor's paws and squeezed them gently. "Don't worry, Clais will be defeated."

"Poor Whisper. We must stop him. I feel sick."

"Come on," Hale said. "Remember our mission, we have work to do which now includes saving Whisper, so we need to move."

Filor's stare broke. "Yes we do, let's go."

They stood together and entered the water. The unseen sandbank descended quickly as they both plunged waist deep into the water. The distance to their sandbank was at least sixty hops away and indicated their exit point at the base of the high red rock. They moved gingerly, placing each paw on the unseen riverbed. They moved loose stones with their paws to ensure a solid pawing and assured balance. The water was angry and forceful as if affronted they would once again dare enter its grasp having escaped multiple times.

"Are you okay?" said Hale who led the way.

"Yeah," said Filor through cold silent gasps.

They both held onto the sandbank for stability as the water worked to pull them back into instability and danger. Hale's mind wondered if the threatening water she had escaped further up the river had once again found her. They rounded the final bend and with the rock wall now a short distance away, a small hollow could be seen in the rock face where they could hide and collect their thoughts before moving along its base. The noise of the troop was now at its loudest and words could now be heard and were clear.

Suddenly, there was a ripping sound. A clump of grass and root Filor was holding onto, broke free and she momentarily lost her pawing. Struggling to grab the bank the water quickly grabbed the opportunity of vulnerability and pulled her from the bank. Her long hind paws scrambled for any sort of balance or traction on the riverbed. The stones she eagerly sought for stability, rolled away as if complicit in the water making good on its threat of revenge.

She fell forward and was briefly submerged albeit briefly and on breaking the surface mouthed a silent, panicked scream. She opened a paw to Hale, with wild panicked eyes.

Hale, having been acutely aware of the situation, had firmed her grip on the bank in preparation for the likely impact of her stretched paw. She dug her claws into a thick root which had multiple tentacles anchored deep within the mud and rock. She leant out and grabbed Filor's paw. With a mighty effort, she swung her back into the bank before letting go. Filor spun to have her chest face the oncoming stream and she straightened her hind legs finding firm pawing on the riverbed. This singular movement flipped the waters anger as it reluctantly pushed against her chest propelling her to a standing position. She quickly turned to her left and grabbed the riverbank foliage with a strong unrelenting grip. The bank welcomed her back, supporting her call for help and held firm. She looked at Hale and after a few deep breaths and a muffled cough, she mouthed, 'Thank you,' with a smile.

Hale, impressed with her acrobatic move, mouthed, 'Wow,' and smiled back with a broad grin.

They continued to make cautious hops along the riverbank, reaching the rock face where they planned their escape. Along the cliff base ran an alcove, deep and dark. It was lower than they expected with craggy overhangs, but it followed a line that would take them back into Balagh. The water in which they now stood, was shallow and the bank remained shoulder high but on a sandy slope which would help their exit. They stood-side-by side and could just about make out the outline of the tree canopy where the Clais troop lay somewhere in the dark.

Hale pushed Filor out of the water who in return pulled Hale free with a concerted effort. The water bubbled and popped as if boiling with rage at letting them go for a third and what would be final time. They quickly moved into the dark hollow and hugged each other to gain warmth whilst they discussed their next move. After a few moments they moved deeper into the darkest crags and recesses. The wind and rain were gaining strength once more. As the wind whistled through, they feared albeit briefly, that the cliff could collapse at any moment, but the ancient rock stood firm. A large slow-moving cloud covered the moon's prying eye and created a deep, impenetrable darkness. The wind abated. However, in its place fell a soaking drizzle which cloaked them in a shroud of invisibility.

In the little light they had left, they stooped and followed the relatively flat sloping wall that descended further into the depths of the overhang. They leant forwards to rest on their front paws. The cold wet rock brushed their sodden heads and the high points in their arched backs. As the moon broke free of the cloud, it highlighted painted drawings on the flat rock surface. Stunned, they stood in silence and absorbed the beauty of the depictions. The drawings were brightly coloured, with thousands of dots and swirls which seemed to portray tall walkers chasing their kin with large sticks and what appeared to be objects being thrown through the air. They also depicted large fish which they both recognised from the billabong, and lizards and snakes like they had seen on hot days at the base of trees. One of the drawings depicted a yellow-eyed snake like the one that had killed King Delanor, Broadback's father.

The drawings, although a little distressing in showing their kin being hunted, were mesmerised by their vivid movements and flow within the story being told. Hale and Filor looked at each other in silence before holding each other's paws for a moment before they turned and headed to their exit point.

On exiting the overhang, they estimated there were only twenty hops from the base of the climb into Balagh. The place Filor had left just two suns ago. For Hale a number for which she had lost count.

Filor took the moment of silence to self-reflect on her experiences on reaching this point and a sense of pride pulsed through her. There was her first hop out onto the flatland, having descended the slope with a pounding heart filled with apprehension and an overwhelming sense of excitement. Laughing with Whisper as they rolled in the wet grass, leaving Whisper as she took her first hop south. Pulling Hale clear of the water and being pulled free of the water by Hale. In those two suns she had confronted situations that in her normal world she would have avoided with a conscious effort to melt away into her surroundings, unseen, unheard and unknown. On this journey she had found an inner strength and a voice worth listening to.

She now felt strong and decisive with a confidence that no matter the challenge she now faced, she would stand and be counted amongst her peers. In a fleeting moment of reflection, an inner pride glowed on what she achieved thus far but with the presence of mind that the most important part of the journey was yet to come.

She took a deep breath with the hope that Whisper was safe and had intercepted the Tronta troop. She also hoped Thulo was safe. Deep down she couldn't wait to hold him tight once more. However, she blocked the thought from developing as she needed to remain focused and alert.

Hale stood silent as if recognizing the reflective moment Filor was having and gave her the opportunity, knowing how important it was for her if they were going to achieve their unified goal. However, she also needed to balance just how little time they had to inform Broadback and implement a plan before the sun rose and the Clais attack began.

After a short pause she mouthed, "Come on," and used her paw to point up the hill and then to the dreary night sky to emphasize the point of being invisible. Turning, they looked back across the open land to the trees as a final check to study the land between them and make sure the entry was free of Clais guards. They studied the steep path to the rocked entrance before turning to face each other where they smiled, gripped each other's paws for a final time with building exhilaration.

Red Dawn Rising

Clais stood alone looking north. He pictured himself standing on the elevated platform in the cave of kings and his etching dominating those who had gone before. His eyes narrowed and a disfigured smile ran across his wide jaw at this fleeting thought. Twinkles filled the fading night sky and Clais smiled broadly. He pictured the confusion Tronta would endure when the alternative slowly dawned upon him. A painful realisation that they had been fooled and Balagh had fallen, their home lost and those they loved murdered and Broadback defeated.

A gentle wind rippled up his back from the south, peaking and troughing as it passed over his noduled muscular back. It wrapped around him like a dark cold cloak and reached his snout before infiltrating his dark nostrils on a deep intake of breath of cold air. He suddenly spun quickly and violently to face the steep climb to Balagh that stood some eighty hops away. He raised his head, took in long deep breaths with flared nostrils. Each quantifying breath taken the maximum amount he could afford. The entrance remained empty and still of any movement. His eyes narrowed as he ran his eyes up and down the height of the rocks on each side of the entrance. He also stared deeply into the narrow under hang which ran at least 150 hops to the river that babbled quietly before his stare broke. He turned and to look briefly north before hopping back to the troop and lay next to a tree with bowed head where he went through the attack plan one last time.

The Warning

Careful not to disturb any loose stone which may alert those below of their existence, Hale and Filor reached the top of the climb. However, the silence of their movement alerted the lizard to intruders and he scurried out from his hiding place to confront the threat. Raising his head, the lizard flicked his tongue rigorously as if picking their scent.

With smiles, Filor and Hale stared at the rock as the lizard's sharp claws scratched the surface. The vigorous bobbing of its head seemed to be in recognition of his excitement at their safe return home.

They descended the track with excited hearts. On reaching the bottom, they sent quick glances left, right and forward where the billabong sat mirrored and calm. All was quiet barring the talk between two naughty chicks high in the tree canopy above them. Looking up the chicks peered over the thickly twigged nest, much to their mother's consternation and she gave them a good telling off.

Hale took a deep breath as she looked upon Balagh. It was even more beautiful than she had memorised all those moons ago. Her only wish was that her father could have been there to have seen it with her.

All of a sudden Broadback loomed from out of the shadows. His movements were slow and purposeful as if readying himself for a fight. Hale, having not seen Broadback for such a long time, swallowed as she had forgotten just how big and intimidating he was, especially when wearing his battle face. His bright blue eye pierced his dark features even from thirty hops away, but as he approached, his features gently softened.

"Filor, Hale," he stammered as though in disbelief before his voice turned more urgent. "Where's Whisper?" He peered back to the climb in which they had descended.

"She went north to find Tronta, Thulo, Gribe and the troop to warn them," Filor said in an urgent but hushed voice.

"Why have you returned and Hale, what are you doing here, where's your father?"

Hale looked up at him with pooling eyes, "He's," she took a deep swallow, "he's dead. He was murdered by Clais, who found out that father was feeding you information about his planned attack. Clais was giving father false information. He was leading him to think they intended to attack through the northern entrance. Clais knew this would be fed back to you and you would send your troops to fortify and defend the opening." She paused to allow Broadback time to absorb the information as he stood staring at her with a heavy frown. "There is no attack to the north. They are here, on the other side of the pass next to the river."

Broadback's features changed to one of anger as he straightened, and in doing so, grew even larger and more menacing. He spoke quickly, but with clarity and authority. "Okay, tell me all you know and don't leave anything out, no matter how small you think the detail might be."

Filor spoke with interjections from Hale. "They travelled the river, reds and greys, two kings with him and around seventy strong. They plan to attack at the rising of the sun and kill everyone." She paused and swallowed, wetting her lips while staring at the skyline which in the vast darkness had a hint of orange at its base. "Bar you and your family from living here." She again paused.

Hale continued. "We heard two reds talking at the river's edge. Once the battle has been fought, they are going to kill all the greys and take Balagh for their own." She finished almost breathless having spoken without pause, her eyes wide and full of apprehension.

Broadback had listened to the briefing with his eye closed and with no interjections as if picturing the story in his mind. Once they had finished there was a long pause, both Hale and Filor looked at each other with equally thick frowns as Broadback stood with his head hung. Suddenly he looked up and they both saw a brilliant flash of light upon opening his eye. It was as if he had played out all the possible scenarios to a conclusion and they both noticed the very briefest of what appeared to be a smile.

"We need to act and act fast as we don't have much time. When did you leave Whisper?"

"Two moons ago," said Filor.

"Let's hope she intercepted them in time and they are on their way back. But we must plan for the worst," said Broadback with a tone of considered thought. "To the east of the billabong there lies a crop of rocks 1000 hops away." He pointed to a high rounded outcrop that stood awkwardly between two sharp pointed ones crests to its left and right.

"Filor," his voice sharp and decisive, "the remaining troops lie in the great cave. Have them meet me at the tree, but you must be quiet. Hale, wake Trola and Siran and have them take the elders and young to Bolparate. We have already practised for such a moment as this. We have stocked the cave with a plentiful supply of food and in there lies a natural spring. It is imperative you stress the need for silence and inform them the order has come from me directly."

With this, Filor moved off quickly and Hale stood by Broadback's side. He turned to look at her and placed a paw on her shoulder. "It's great to see you again, Hale. You have done your father proud." He moved to hold her small paw in his large pad.

"I miss him so much" said Hale, "but I am glad to be home."

Broadback gave a small smile. "This will always be your home but right now we have work to do." He lifted his head to the moon which was now lost in the lower branches of the silver tree directly overhead. Broadback noted its move across the sky appeared to be slower than normal. It was as if the moon was reluctant to allow the sun to rise, knowing that when it rose again, all it had known might be lost. In the distant horizon the dark night sky was being replaced with the tipping of the new day's sun, completely oblivious to danger upon which it was about to shine its light.

"Right," Broadback said, "it's time for you to go. I want you to follow the elders and look after the young as they surely can be a handful. I want you both to lead the group firstly to Bolporate, then southwards to Landar. The boomers there are our close friends and will look after you."

"No," said Hale, in a defiant tone. "We have not travelled all this way to hide. I would rather die fighting than hide when Balagh faces its greatest ever threat."

"No" said Broadback, "you must guide those who are at most risk. I don't want further unnecessary bloodshed and loss of life to our family."

Hale found her voice, looking Broadback directly in the eye. "You said we are as brave as any warrior you have ever known. Therefore, we stay and fight," with a tone of finality.

Broadback paused and eyed her, his initial sternness as their king, moved to an expression of resounding love, admiration and finally resignation. He leant forward and placed his large paw on Hale's shoulder. "You are just like your father. A true and unwavering friend to me and the vision we jointly held for Balagh. Loving, loyal and as tough as they come and one whom I would have entrusted my life. I would have been proud to stand next to him in any battle and I would be equally proud to stand next to you as his daughter in facing this evil threat." He straightened and smiled. "Let me tell you my plan and what we need to do to prepare. Follow me." They moved off closely huddled in discussion and entered the large cave where they disappeared into the darkness of its shadows.

I've Been Expecting You

Clais had not slept. He stood near the high entrance to Balagh as the moon dipped and the sun peaked, casting shadows and light across his deep-set features as he turned to face the dawning day. To his left, twenty-five greys and reds gathered and patted each of their own kin on the backs. The greys noticeably less enthusiastic than the reds. The energy was building, particularly in the reds selected for the first wave. They were hardened, aggressive, solitary individuals. They gathered around Clais, grunting as steam rose from their backs and held as if a cloud in the early morning cold. He continued his stare to the large V-shaped rocks as if he could see through them and visualise the scene of unprepared calm on the other side. He knew Broadback would be exposed, vulnerable and alone. No matter how fierce a warrior he was, without Tronta and his troop, he would be defeated. The death of Clais' father would be avenged and his promise to his dying father met.

He turned to his boomers with a stony face and hard glare. His scarred lip was red, inflamed and bleeding through chewing the rubbery tissue throughout the night. His jaw pulsed rhythmically and at the end of his broad snout sat dark deep-set eyes, which penetrated from under a thick frown of bristly fur.

"I expect you to do exactly what I have asked, no more, no less. Everyone who is not a blood relative to Broadback is to die: old, young, male, female. The Broadback bloodline and those who call him king ends today."

These words further heightened those who crowded close.

"Broadback and his family are mine and must not be harmed." The demand finished with a deep rumbling hiss. "Go now, your new home awaits and today we celebrate victory in blood, together red and grey alike."

With these words the warriors became even more agitated with pulsating excitement, eyes glazed with hatred and murder. They turned and hopped quickly to the entrance, each jostling to be the first through the narrow gap. Each wanted to take the first deep, clawed strike, the first to taste blood, the first to murder.

They scrambled up the steep embankment, some passing others as they jostled and slipped in their eagerness to be first. Breathless, they arrived at the top and quickly navigated the narrow track which had been laid out in their attack plans. Two of the boomers tried to pass those in front before they slipped and tumbled down the bank. One stifled the pain as his leg snapped with a loud crack. The other lay motionless and silent, having hit his head. Blood oozed from his snout and ear.

The remainder moved too fast around the narrow bend and tumbled down the steep bank to the flat lands of Balagh scrambling to gain their stance in front of the billabong. The others, on arriving at the levelled surface, stood looking around with spittle foaming in their thick fibrous chin fur. Each breathing hard, each shaking with adrenalin-fuelled anticipation. Each wanted the chase, each wanting the kill.

However, Balagh lay empty. A gentle breeze rippled the surface of the water which lapped gently on the sandy bank. The birds in the treetop nests peered down in silence. The only audible sound was their laboured breaths which were fuelled by surging adrenalin. They stood stock still and confused as the sun sat proud on the distant horizon and cast their shadows long and thin in the orange sand.

A sound drew their attention. They turned to face the large boab tree. Before it stood a huge figure.

A murmur ran through the waiting troop.

"Broadback," one stammered as he bounced nervously.

Filor and Hale moved from the wide tree base to stand either side of Broadback. All three were cast in the shadows of the large tree's huge wide limbs.

The Clais troop faced them. Instinctively, the reds scratched the sand with thick claws and expelled deep, menacing grunts. The lead of the red troop, Valant, hopped forward. He was older than the rest of the reds who remained stationary, the greys to their rear and noticeably silent.

Valant stood tall with a medium frame. Once muscled, his fur hung loose around his midriff that was patched in areas across his chest with little scars. He held an air of arrogance and superiority and a noticeable odour of travel.

"Broadback" he said with sarcasm, "good to see you."

Broadback recognized him from the last battle. "You're still alive then, but only just by the look and smell of you."

The boomers who stood just to the rear of Valant, snorted and went to move forward but Valant raised a paw and they stopped.

"Clais wants you and your family for himself. Come quietly and save the slaughter of the ones who you claim to love. A true king would not see the death of his own. He would step forward and accept his inevitable fate."

Valant turned to the boomers at his rear with a smug glare as if making the point. He paused to see what Broadback's reaction would be.

When Broadback remained stationary and unfazed, Valant continued. "You cannot win, Broadback. Surely you can see that. You are outnumbered. Your troop is days away on a false belief we would attack to the north and you have nowhere to hide."

At these words, Broadback reached out for Filor and Hale, his paws dwarfing theirs in size. He gripped them gently before he let them go. "Stay here, that's an order." He hopped forward, giving no time for a riposte and turned to face them both. They were silent but their faces expressed more than words could have. "I must do this and I order you as your King, to stay right here. I will plead with Clais for your lives to be spared." He spun around on his thick tail and slowly hopped forward.

Having heard the words spoken to both Filor and Hale Valant stood tall with a sneer. However, when Broadback took his final hop to stand in front of him, Valant swallowed deep and licked his lips.

Broadback studied the boomers who stood some seven hops behind, his scar ablaze in red and orange reflecting the early morning light. The confidence they showed when he stood at the Boab was now less evident as they twitched and peeked at each other, now towering over them.

"Come," said Valant in a soft patronising voice, "you are doing the right thing. You have spared lives, have conceded that you cannot …"

Before Valant could speak his last word, Broadback lunged forward and grabbed Valant by the neck. In one swift movement he lifted Valant off the ground to his height and yanked him forward. Broadback glowered straight into Valant's eyes and with a quick spin, cracked Valant's neck with an echoing force before he dropped him dead to the ground.

The greys and reds staggered around in shock, leaving Broadback standing motionless. They shot quick glances at each other in silent questions. If one was to attack would the rest follow? Whilst confusion grew there was a change in their immediate surroundings. The birds who had been silent, started to squawk. Life in the billabong suddenly ignited into raucous noise. Unseen insects hummed a symphony.

Broadback moved forward within striking range of the greys and reds. He hopped slowly, with obvious purpose, up and down their line, eyeing each with an unwavering air of authority. Agitated and distressed, they sent out loud snorting grunts. Fear etched across their faces, some urinated as they stared beyond Broadback's glare.

Broadback slowly turned. Standing some ninety hops away and slightly elevated on a rock shelf, stood some eighty battle-hardened boomers. At the head of the troop stood Tronta, Thulo, Gribe and Whisper. To their right stood Lombard and the kings from the east and south. The reds in front of Broadback slowly shuffled, eager to reach the steep climb from which they emerged and return to Clais and relative safety.

The resulting silence was deafening, Tronta raised his paw. Tronta's boomers moved as one to block the exit. This strategic move effectively extinguishing their only hope of escape. The greys and reds began to huddle into their respective groups. Each looking at the other in mistrust and suspicion.

Broadback hopped forward and addressed them. "You have been led here under false pretences. Clais has betrayed you." He pointed to the troop of greys who stood huddled in a concave within the rock face. "Clais plans to kill you all and take Balagh for his own."

The greys eyed each other in shock. Heads turned to Broadback and back to the reds.

As the Tronta troop edged forward, the reds shuffled along the base of the rock face in a thinned gaped line, all unity gone. At its distal end there was a promise of open land but only with the very slimmest chance of escape.

Broadback hopped forward and stood in front of the greys, his body language offering one of peace. "I have no war intentions with you. I understand your land is desperate and you have the need for water and food and the promise of a better life for you and your families. But this is not the way. Let's work together in partnership where we will be stronger. Where we are unified as one. We welcome you and your kin to our land. We can share our resources and live in harmony. In our history we have never fought the greys and we do not wish for that to change. I will spare your lives if you withdraw from this fight. I will work with your king as an equal once Clais is defeated." He opened his arms wide in welcome. "What do you say?"

The greys looked at each other and after a brief discussion there came a voice from the group. "My name is Drogoll and I speak for us all. We live in harsh times. We have been forced to take this action against our will due to lack of water and food. Clais would not allow free passage across his borders to meet with you. With the threat of starvation, we had little option but to join him. I speak for all greys when I say none of us wanted to fight or be part of any murderous killing. We respect Balagh and the kings who have ruled this land with fairness and empathy. I knew your father Delanor, to be a respectful and a very fair king to the hardships of the land. Therefore, we accept your offer of reprieve and the open paw of friendship and respect."

Broadback hopped forward, stood in front of Drogoll and placed his paws on his shoulders. He stooped to butt his forehead to that of Drogoll, the offer of safe passage sealed. After a momentary pause, Drogoll hopped back to sit in the shade of the hollow with his troop and looked on towards the reds.

Broadback now turned to face the reds. His vivid blue eye dark as he stood to his fullest height. "You have always wreaked havoc on our lands, sought to destroy those who offer the paw of friendship. You have all supported Clais' threats of destruction, disharmony, murder, dictatorship, self-worth and self-preservation and fed from his blooded paw. You will always seek chaos over harmony and will never leave the lands to grow and prosper." His voice darkened. "As such, you are untrustworthy and will not be spared." He fell silent before hopping forward. "As you would not have spared my family."

At these words the reds took flight in differing directions in clear, unthought panic. Their actions demonstrated self-preservation at the very forefront of their individual thinking. Tronta waved his arm forward and his troop moved quickly. The evidence of their training was on clear display as they hopped in pairs, in perfect unison as if one, living, breathing being. As each of the reds was caught, they were mercilessly taken to the ground. Hind legs kicked from under them with a practised sweep. On hitting the ground, the second boomer stomped on the exposed unprotected neck. The pain felt would have been minimal. The marauder dispatched with ruthless efficiency. Most offered little more than a panicked grunt or pleading word. Tronta moved amongst the dead, a line of red mud taken from the billabong bank pawed across their backs and snouts to signify they were deceased. Those who Tronta came across trying to escape were killed and marked, their pleas for mercy ignored.

Filor and Hale stood with Whisper. They hugged each other in a tight embrace. Warm tears flowed, each filled with excitement, love and laughter as they pawed each other for any unseen injury they may have received on their travels. After a brief discussion, they turned to face the brutality and were overcome by an unexpected sadness. The stench of death and fear filled the air. They wondered if those who lay dead had been inherently violent, nasty and ruthless. Or had they believed Clais' rhetoric and false promises of wealth and status? Had they been brainwashed into attacking Balagh for a life that in reality, would never have existed under his cruel narcissistic rule?

Broadback hopped to join the kings from the west and south. As he did so, they leant forward and touched foreheads as a sign of respect and loyalty to one another.

Broadback hopped to Lombard and met his head in a prolonged touch of foreheads. They talked while holding each other's shoulders firmly. On separating, Lombard looked skywards and moved off alone with tears flowing. Thulo and Gribe moved to join Broadback, who raised his arms and placed them around the shoulders of his sons.

"Good timing," he said with a smile.

"Just as we planned," said Gribe, looking at Thulo, before embracing him in a firm hug.

Broadback pulled them in close and they were momentarily held helpless under his arms which spanned them both.

Upon their release Thulo asked, "What about Clais?"

Before he could answer he was embraced in a tight hug. Whisper beamed up at him, excitement ablaze in her eyes.

"Hello, father."

"Hello, Whisper," he said. "Who's been busy then?" He smiled. "I am so, so proud of you and I look forward to hearing all about your adventures later, however this is not over yet."

He turned to face them all. "I need to end this evil and free us of this tyranny and threat."

Their faces were framed in worried concern, each having no doubt what he meant.

"Do not worry yourselves. By the day's end, Balagh will be free and we can celebrate all we have and love."

He moved off with Tronta to join the troop who had once again lined up to stand in perfect uniformity. Near the far wall lay a pile of lifeless twisted bodies stacked high, bloodied and broken. Shadowed shapes crossed the sand upon which they stood as high in the torrents of unseen wind, large birds with silent wings circled, hungry for a free meal.

Without further words, Broadback hopped off in the direction of the tree, followed by Tronta who knew this action was a request to join him. They moved in silence, passing the greys who stood and bowed their heads as a show of respect. Both Broadback and Tronta did the same.

Under the shadow of a large limb, Tronta spoke. "What is the plan?"

"I must face Clais alone," said Broadback. "This has been foretold since the death of his father. I must be the one to battle him as our lands can never move forward whilst he lives. The greys are to be spared, the remaining reds who are massed on the other side are to be shown no mercy. Clais is there awaiting the command of Valant, in the assumption that I have been captured. Move the troops to the open land. Block any escape and force his troops to the river. None are to escape. Use the hidden route to the east and await my command."

Tronta and Broadback turned to face each other. They reached out and gripped each other's forearm before pulling each other into a firm embrace. Words were not needed. As they went to separate, Tronta momentarily gripped Broadback's arm. "Rid us of this evil once and for all, show no mercy and give no quarter."

Clais

The entrance to the top of the slope remained eerily silent. Clais squinted as the sun moved to its midpoint on its climb and the heat was building. Phase one should have been completed by now and Broadback should have been beaten and bloodied by this point in the sun's arc.

The remaining reds and greys shuffled impatiently as the heat rose. A flock of noisy birds took flight from the sightless billabong. They flew in a circular display before descending at speed and landing in the high foliage of the trees under which the Clais troop stood. As the birds landed high upon the high branches, they fell silent as if knowing what was to come.

The boomers watched their flight in silence before returning their mesmerised gaze to the opening at the top of the steep bank. Suddenly each stiffened at the sound of a booming voice. It filled the valley from upon high.

"I am the rightful king of Balagh. You enter my land not as friends but as marauders, murderers and sneaks." Broadback appeared between the two V-shaped rocks.

Clais gasped and momentarily shuffled on his long hind paws before standing firm. The reds snorted in shock and for most fear. The absence of those who had ascended and entered Balagh on the rising of the sun, could only mean they had been killed.

Broadback spoke in the deafening silence. "You are not welcome here and you will be punished. I speak to the greys and the greys only. Your comrades have been spared death as you have all been fooled by Clais and his impotent lies. I will spare you if you do not take arms against me and work with me in an allegiance of trust and honesty. I promised your leader, Drogoll, who now sits in Balagh unharmed. We have jointly agreed the freedom to live a prosperous life with us. On this you have my word."

Clais stared up with rising rage. Bubbles of phlegm grew and his neck and chest became quickly soaked in the uncontrolled dribble and rising sweat.

"What do you say,"? said Broadback.

The greys bowed their heads in unison and headed to the shaded solitude of the trees.

"If what you say is the truth," Clais yelled "then the greys are no great loss. They are not equal to us." He studied the tree where they now massed. "They are weak, small and easy to manipulate. When you are dead, Broadback, the reprieve you have given them will be meaningless to me. They will be killed without mercy and I will rule all the lands under a position of strength, not weakness." He did not look at the greys who now stared at him from under the shaded canopy of the tree. "But how did you learn of our massing to the east?" Clais asked.

Broadback smiled. "Loyalty and bravery, qualities you would not understand. This finishes today. If you want revenge for your father's death and Balagh for your rule, I stand alone." He hopped from the entrance and disappeared out of sight.

Clais' eyes narrowed to slits as a smile crept across his contorted face.

His brothers moved forward, "Don't go, Clais. It's clearly a trap."

Clais turned to them. "You do not say this out of concern or love for me. You advise this because you are weak and you fear death. You want me to stay and protect you. You are nothing but an embarrassment to me as you were to our father. Go and join the greys as they are all you are worthy of. I'll deal with you later."

He turned to the empty entrance. "When I take Broadback's life, I will rule this land alone and only the loyal will stand by my side." He placed a paw on Blont's shoulder, who stood separate from his brothers. Clais turned and ascended the incline with purpose. Each bound was powerful and purposeful and disappeared into the opening.

Eye to Eyes

Clais entered the opening. The red dirt upon which he hopped was firm. A few protruding rocks peaked out like capped heads swimming in a pool filled with sand. The sun had moved overhead, and the wafting breeze was warm.

Broadback stood at the far end, motionless, his blue eye laser sharp and focused.

Clais moved into the space and paced back and forth, mouthing his lower jaw as drool streamed thickly and glistened in the sun. "You have made a fatal mistake facing me Broadback. I don't need those others to kill you. You're old, slow and tired." He spelled each word out in a slow, pointed manner. With a glance to the opening, he continued. "They are weak. They do not have what it takes to kill, to take a life. They do not have what it takes to rule and command without question." He continued to pace with blazing eyes. "Since taking my father's life, you must have known I would take yours, take from you what you have taken from me. When you are beaten, disabled, pathetic, I will kill your family and you will watch as your bloodline ends except for your precious daughter Whisper, who will bear my children." He made a deep barrelled laugh.

Broadback stood unmoved, knowing that Clais was trying to unsettle him and act without thought or control.

Clais continued to speak in various pitches, spittle bright white, his eyes narrowed, his ears folded back.

Broadback stood calm and spoke in a measured tone. "You are not fit to rule. You are untrustworthy and your narrow view of the lands is not one of humbleness, joy or possibilities but one of destruction and misery. Your world is full of hatred, mistrust and loneliness. I cannot let those values rule. You must see that."

While Broadback had been talking, Clais had edged slowly forward. When Broadback finished, Clais rounded and lunged forward with surprising agility. The distance between them seemed to fold as if time itself was halved. Within striking distance, Clais fell back on his thick muscular tail and lunged his rear clawed paws with the intent of tearing at Broadback's abdomen.

Broadback side-hopped the attack and deflected the blow.

Clais skidded on the ground and turned quickly in preparation for the inevitable counterattack.

However, Broadback hopped off slowly with his back turned before he spun on his tail to face Clais again. He remained calm, measured with his breathing slow and controlled.

Clais smiled, zig-zagged forward to reduce the angle for another Broadback escape. He closed the distance quickly and again leant back on his thick tail.

Broadback leant back to once again deflect the blow.

Clais lunged forward using his powerful tail and hind legs to propel him. With a distinctive height advantage and momentum, he landed a blow square on the side of Broadback's snout.

The impact knocked Broadback to the ground before he scrambled to stand again to face Clais. Blood pooled in his mouth. With a smile, he spat out a tooth which rolled and sat in a large sandy clot.

"Didn't see that coming, did you?" Clais said with a wry smile, making reference to having one eye. Before he could finish his drooling laugh, Broadback covered the distance between them in two bounds and landed a blow to Clais' right eye.

Clais spun with the impact. His eye closed quickly as blood poured from the broken socket. Clais turned and roared in anger, facing Broadback once more and clawed the ground with his powerful hind legs.

"Now we fight evenly," said Broadback with a spit of blood onto the now gnarled and uneven ground.

They circled each other, each alert for any miniscule twitch or sign of another attack.

The lizard stood rigid, bouncing on his front legs, tongue twitching rapidly with a concerned expression across his face. The sun was high and their resulting shadows cast by were contorted and disfigured as they circled each other. Clais lunged forward, locking arms. Both bared and bit with their teeth.

Broadback deflected Clais' bite with his forehead, the strike clearly aimed at his throat.

Clais latched onto Broadback's ear which he pulled and ripped, before jerking away.

Broadback staggered back with blood surging and running down his face.

Clais spat the piece of gristle out which rolled into the sand.

Broadback pawed the wound and rubbed the blood away from his eye, the empty socket filling fast from the constant stream.

Clais took the opportunity of distraction to launch another attack.

Broadback stooped in anticipation and hopped to the side as Clais passed by with his aggressive, weighted momentum. Broadback sunk his claws into Clais' exposed abdomen and pulled hard which ripped the soft tissue into ragged lines.

Clais grimaced in pain and immediately placed his paws over the wound before he dared to look up and snarl.

"You bleed just like your father," said Broadback.

"Don't you dare speak his name," roared Clais.

Both breathing heavy, they circled each other, adrenalin pumping through their bodies. A slight twitch from Clais gave away his intended move and they both met in the middle of the clearing. Each had wide stances for maximum power. Both landed equal blows with outstretched claws. As they separated, Clais landed a final blow, which struck Broadback's snout. The result was like an explosion as it bled profusely. He looked up. Clais stood with a twisted smile. His eye was now completely swollen; his abdominal wound streaked in red with exposed flesh. They circled once more before lunging again. Broadback crouched under the swinging arms and landed a heavy blow to Clais' abdomen and upwards under his jaw. This assault knocked Clais' head backwards. Phlegm and blood cast skywards before splatting on the sand and rock which encircled them. Clais staggered backwards. His arms dropped and he sagged.

After landing the blow, Broadback prepared to land the winning strike to the defenceless, dazed Clais. As he did so his rear hind paw stood on an unseen, uneven rock. Losing his balance, he fell sideways and landed heavily on his shoulder.

In an instant, Clais regained his equilibrium and moved forward, raising a rear leg with the clear intent of stamping hard. The strike was clearly aimed at Broadback's now exposed neck.

Instinctively, Broadback raised his arm and although he deflected the blow, a loud snap was heard.

Whisper couldn't bear to watch as she hugged Filor tight. They stood in the shadows of the rock wall, peering around the only bend in the narrow path before the clearing. The same bend where her brother Gribe had stood when she and Thulo had discussed that he might be in line to be King when their father relinquished the crown.

Peering between a low point in the wall they looked upon Tronta, who stood alone, paw deep in the billabong. His reflection ebbed and flowed and contorted in the gentle ripple that ran across its surface. Filor could not believe that Balagh and their way of life was about to end, with her father's death. That the reds and Clais would soon stand on her sand, wash their smelly fur in her water and stand in the cave of kings which was a beacon of continued hope for them all. Although Tronta would undoubtedly fight to the very end, it had been agreed with her father that negotiation and the sparing of lives was the priority. It had been agreed with the kings who now stood in arms with them, they would take the young and elderly back to their lands. Tronta fully expected to lose his life as part of any agreed negotiation and Whisper would likely have to stay until all those who were vulnerable were safe.

As Whisper's thoughts frantically came and went the realisation of her predicament was broken by the most awful of sounds. She had never heard her father in pain or seen him cry. She instinctively firmed her stance at the sound of breaking bone albeit brief. She felt Filor grip her tight and put her head on Filor's shoulder, having looked away from the unfolding scene.

On the platform in the cave, Thulo heard the unmistakable sound of his father's cry of pain, followed by a deafening silence. He turned and eyed the high wall that depicted his family's line of kings, from his father and his father's, father. He wished he had known them all. Wished that he too could have joined them one day and wondered how he would have led and been remembered as King of Balagh. Staring up, he saw himself etched upon the wall standing next to his father. A king known for his integrity, one with compassion and shared growth and optimism and one offering the hand of friendship across the great open lands. On this thought he turned back to the distant shimmer, no longer a stranger, no longer something to be feared in its vastness but simply a gateway to opportunity. He saw himself standing next to

Filor with her hopping around after a young buck who was trying to escape her clutches, who was chasing his sister who was sticking her tongue out at him. He smiled warmly at this thought which was vanquished when Tronta came into the cave.

"We need to talk," he said with an air of resignation.

Broadback peered into the narrowed eyes of Clais which were dark. Spittle sprayed as he spoke unheard words through rasping breaths. The pain in his shoulder stabbed. His breathing was difficult through a nose blocked with clotted blood. His arm seared with heat as the broken bones ground in its free swing. Clais' breath was stale and rotten; the smell of anger and evil could almost be tasted.

Suddenly a warm silence filled Broadback's inner thoughts as he prepared himself for the end. As he looked at the still mouthing Clais, he was blinded by a glint, like a brightly shining star. In the calmness and silence of his thoughts, he was taken to a vision of Olan.

"There you are," she said, her voice soft, confident and flowing, just as he had remembered. The light flickered behind her and out of it came Olan's soft open paw which invited him to join her. He pushed himself up. As he reached for her. He no longer had a broken arm, painful shoulder and looked upon her beauty with not one eye but two. She pulled him up effortlessly into a warm embrace. She nestled into him and the warmth and smell of her fur was as if it was the first time they had embraced all those beautiful suns and moons ago under the silvery bark of the boab.

Loosening her embrace, she said, "Don't be afraid. Where I am now is so beautiful. I am with your father and grandfather, grandchildren and friends who have passed over. I have a beautiful home, and we have so many friends who share love and freedom. Our land is free of any war or division. We live and love as you had always hoped. You will love it here," smiling "but not yet Broadback." Her voice firmed as she stared up at him. "Your life's mission in Balagh has not yet been fulfilled. All of those who you love; Whisper, Thulo, Tronta and those who call you king, need you now more than they ever have. We will be together again. It has been foretold, but you have a responsibility to fight."

"But I want to be with you again, now," he said. The glinting light pierced his closed eyelid as Olan's paw vanished from where it had come. He slowly opened his eye. The pain from which he had been relieved in Olan's presence had returned with an uncompromising vengeance. But worse, he was looking up and facing the contorted smile of Clais who was in striking distance. Death filling Clais' deep, dark, piercing stare.

Two Whistles, Blank Eyes, Wide Eyes

With the briefest of whistles, the impacting thud was violent and hollow. The blood sprayed outward from Clais' chest like a large stone being dropped into water. Fur, muscle and tissue hung loose upon the projectile's exit. As quickly as the first had hit, a second appeared a blink later, higher up but equally as powerful and devastating. Clais looked down in uncertain disbelief, his prior expression of hate was replaced with shock and confusion in his contorted features. His last gasps were fluid filled gurgles as blood poured unabated from the open wounds. Coughing a frothed spittle bubbled with each rasp and ran from his contorted mouth. He tried to grab Broadback who had slumped to the ground but missed with a flailing paw and a grunted deflating hiss.

He rasped for breath. All fight and anger seeped out of his open wounds. He blinked rapidly and there in front of him stood his father, who was silent, his face as he remembered it; hard, uncompromising with no love or concern at his son's life-ending predicament. His father's face was etched with disappointment at his failure. Clais staggered towards the opening. For the briefest of moments, he seemed to raise both arms as if waiting to be held, to be embraced.

Clais' father did not hop forward to meet his loving request in his final rasps. Clais simply wanted to be held, to be told it was going to be okay, that his father was proud of him and loved him. However, his father remained passive, unmoved and with a final look of disgust turned and hopped back into the darkness from where he had came.

Clais' legs sagged. He looked skywards before falling forwards. He tumbled down the bank to lie dead. His head lolled and hung limp across a rock. His dead eye remained wide and if his brain continued to provide sight he would have seen the bodies of his troop laying scattered and bloodied across the basin floor. Their clear direction of travel towards the river as a means of escape futile as Tronta's battle hardened boomers showed no mercy in their killing.

Memories Made

George slowly stood with a few groans. Lying on the hard ground had stiffened his joints. "We got him," he said, patting down his clothes. Orange dust plumbed off with each forceful pat and he coughed.

Bob stood next to him, smiling, his stomach rumbling at having missed breakfast. "Right, one final meal before we head home tomorrow." There was clear satisfaction in his voice.

"Yes, I think we deserve it," said George.

"Thank goodness you missed the intended target, Dad, or we would be eating for months."

"What are you talking about? The one I aimed for is the one I hit."

They both looked back down the winding path to their makeshift camp site. "What you should never do, son, is go home with any food or beer. That, my son, would be a mission failure."

"So true and it's your turn to cook tonight," said Bob with his back turned and zipping up the rifle bag before throwing it over his shoulder and walking off towards the car.

George finished his stretch earlier than his body requested at this unbelievable statement, his arms slumping to his side, "I cooked last night. It's your turn, I cook, you wash."

"How tall do you think he was?" shouted Bob.

"Oh at least eleven feet tall. That's what I will tell the grandkids."

"Bloody ugly too. It looked like he had been shot long before we came along, with all the scarring on its face."

"Well, that, my son, was an awesome trip. Your grandad would have loved to have been with us," Bob noticing his father tearing up. "He has been with us this entire time," said Bob. "I have felt his presence throughout this trip dad. He is all around us and I know that he has loved every moment".

As a reflective silence fell between them a large turquoise and black butterfly fluttered down and sat high on a wafting, budding flower. They both looked at each other and smiled, "there he is, I told you he is with us" said Bob and placed a warm hand and gentle squeeze to his father's shoulder.

Standing, Bob stretched and patted dust from his jeans. "I can't wait until next year's trip," pausing, "but think I'll come on my own as I reckon you're just about the right age to join the bowling brigade."

"My arse, I am." shouted George looking offended. "Count me in."

They both laughed and headed down the winding track. Their final laughs were veiled in a shimmer as a curtain of sand blew across the scene, removing their tracks as the sun moved towards the horizon, no doubt looking forward to a rest after the day's exhausting events.

Beaten But Not Broken

Broadback stood holding his arm, blood thick and dry in his nose, his fur sticky around his ripped ear. He gingerly hopped to the edge of the ravine having witnessed the tall walker's departure. He looked down with the sun now low on his back. Clais lay deformed and lifeless, his underbelly exposed with his head and neck stretched over a large rock as the muscles slowly relaxed.

Broadback's gaze broke. He studied the narrow ravine where the Clais troop lay sporadically scattered with no sign of any unified defence mounted. Those who did put up a fight, lay with twisted limbs and their heads lying at unnatural angles. Some of the Broadback troop had started the gruesome task of moving the bodies away from the site. They piled them together under the deep cliff overhang where the drawings lay vibrant and dancing in the shadows.

One of the troop turned and raised his paw into the air. Broadback's large frame silhouetted against the descending sun to his rear, cast his shadow across them all as if an embracing them with heartfelt thanks for their loyalty. Those who carried the dead, put them down and turned to face him.

Broadback recognised Trigor, Groft and Lombard. They all clenched their paws and thumped their chests making loud grunts before bowing their heads. Broadback waited until they all faced him before he bowed his head and beat his chest, his arm hanging limp. He raised his good arm into the air with a clenched paw.

Broadback then turned and made his way back to the billabong, with slow hops down the bank to the water's edge. As he stepped out, Whisper and Thulo appeared, both crying with abandoned relief. The billabong was now a chorus of sound with the birds and insects singing in joyful unity.

"Father are you all alright.?"

"Yeah, a little sore. Watch my arm," he said as she embraced him tightly.

"Is … is he dead?" asked Thulo.

Broadback paused and swallowed. "Yes he is. It's over." His voice wavered as he looked across the billabong and pulled them both in close. To his right stood the solitary figure of Tronta leaning nonchalantly against the base of the boab as if he didn't have a care in the world. Smiling, Broadback clenched his paw, placed it over his heart and pumped his chest gently. Tronta turned and hopped off to where Hale stood. He put his arm around her and placed a kiss on top of her head.

Friendships Forged

Over the following days, life returned to relative normality. The broader family returned from hiding, the young played in the Billabong, disappointed the adventure was over and that teachings had once again begun. Gribe sat with Broadback and the kings of the greys and those from the south and west. They sat close, ate and laughed with each other and departed to warm embraces and future promises. They all agreed to welcome each with open paws and hearts and allow free movement between their lands. The kings agreed that Broadback's proposed competition, *Unshackled*, would commence and be celebrated at each of their respective homes on the cooling of the weather. The premise that the games would consist of a series of both physical and mental challenges with the ultimate winner being named, *Champion Of The Freelands Of Balagh* and would open to both male and females over the age of three years.

Broadback also had the etchings of Whisper, Hale, Filor and Lombard placed onto the wall directly opposite the kings in the great caves. Each stood equal and shoulder-to-shoulder consigning their bravery to history. Broadback also met with the new leaders of the north to forge a relationship that would be prosperous and respectful and offered his land freely in times of hardship.

Hale joined Tronta in teaching the new boomers the art of fighting and the trickier art of stealth. It is told Tronta was often seen smiling warmly at Hale, revelling in her enthusiasm and fearlessness in engagement and that he grew to love her as the daughter he never had.

Thulo and Filor stood on the high plain looking out towards the opening, paw-in-paw. "I am so proud of you," said Thulo.

They turned to face each other and embraced. They laughed as they looked down into Filor's pouch and there.

Nestled deep was a small pink joey. Crouching, Thulo placed his paws on either side and looked up smiling, speaking softly to his newborn. Standing, he placed a gentle kiss on her forehead before embracing in loving silence.

The lizard sat watching before being distracted by the scraping of claws. Turning, he looked at a distant rock where another smaller lizard bobbed on front legs with keen enthusiasm. Their tongues flicked in unison and although hard to tell within their scaly triangular heads, they appeared to be smiling at each other. The newcomer stopped bobbing, flicked its tongue before scuttling off.

Thulo and Filor smiled, having watched the show and with a final look at them both, the lizard turned and scuttled off in pursuit.

As Filor and Thulo looked north, the eyes of Blont watched from the west. Hidden in the shadows next to the river, they were the same cold eyes as his dead brother. Three gnarly boomers stood with him under a low overhang. Each stooped, breathing slow and hard and staring with darkness greater than that which hid them. Turning and unseen, they disappeared and headed across the river to a waiting group. After a brief discussion they moved off and disappeared through the swaying scrub. Blont was left crouching alone. "Enjoy it while you can, worse is yet to come as one will betray you." He smiled before turning and disappearing into the darkness.

Road Trip

"It's hot today," Steve said as Paul went over to the A\C and fired up the old white machine which rattled to life on the wall and coughed out cold air after a spurt of dry dust. They removed their hard hats, placed them next to the sink and picked up a stewed tea. Steve spooned four sugars into a dark brown stained mug and threw the spoon into the sink which clanged with the others that filled the base. Tea marks stained the lettering which read, 'Old Fart, Been There, Seen It and Done It,' which was embossed on the side in discoloured white lettering. As they walked to the old map, the floor bounced in the hastily raised porta cabin. Ripped vinyl with brown and orange chequered squares covered the floor and, in its undulation sat small piles of gritted sand. The map had been placed under a thick Perspex sheet on a wide square table.

"Right," said Paul, pointing to small black stars drawn onto the new brightly coloured map, "the drill holes showed good gold running the entire length of our testing."

"When do the machines arrive?" asked Steve,

"The day after tomorrow and the crew over the coming weeks to capacity over the next six months," said Paul.

"What's the go with the billabong?" asked Steve, pointing.

"I'm not sure. I plan to head out there in a few months to look at its viability. It may give us a good indicator to any water channels that may head this way."

"But we will gain the necessary permits and have permission from the traditional landowners before we do anything."

"I'll come with you if it means me getting out of here for a few hours," said Steve.

They walked over to their computers and began to type, Paul looking out of his orange dusty window to a large, outcropped wall in the far-off distance. He was lost in thought for a few moments before slurping his tea.

"Struth." Opening his drawer, he retrieved a packet of biscuits and dunked one deep. He turned to his keyboard and started tapping on the faded buttons. Friday 28th Proposed Meeting: 0800-1600 - drive to Billabong. Send. A distant ping was heard from the adjoining PC and an 'accepted' ping was instantly received.